COMING TO TERMS

Coming to Terms
A Literary Response to Abortion

EDITED BY

Lucinda Ebersole

AND

Richard Peabody

THE NEW PRESS · NEW YORK

Published in the United States by The New Press, New York
Distributed by W. W. Norton & Company, Inc.,
500 Fifth Avenue, New York, NY 10110

Library of Congress Cataloging in Publication Data

Coming to terms: a literary response to abortion / edited by
Lucinda Ebersole and Richard Peabody.
        p.   cm.
    Includes bibliographical references (p. 181).
    ISBN 1–56584–187–5
        1. Abortion—Fiction. 2. American fiction.   I.
Ebersole, Lucinda.   II. Peabody, Richard, 1951–   .
PS649.A2C65 1995   94–5400
813'.0108356 — DC20

Established in 1990 as a major alternative to the large, commercial
publishing houses, The New Press is the first full-scale nonprofit
American book publisher outside of the university presses. The Press
is operated editorially in the public interest, rather than for private
gain; it is committed to publishing in innovative ways works of edu-
cational, cultural, and community value that, despite their intellec-
tual merits, might not normally be "commercially" viable. The New
Press's editorial offices are located at the City University of New York.

Printed in the United States of America

94 95 96 97   9 8 7 6 5 4 3 2 1

TO MY COEDITOR

*Had it not've been for
the Cotton-Eyed Joe,
I'd have been married
a long time ago.*

TRADITIONAL

Contents

Acknowledgments

Special thanks to Laura Levin for the title;
to the Pho gang; and to Harriet Barlow,
Sara de Saussure Davis, Kitty Gillman, Sharon Henry,
Elaine Orr, Tracey O'Shaughnessy,
Nancy Taylor, and C. Jenise Williamson.

Preface

Abortion!

It screams at us from the covers of *Time* and *Newsweek,* from the steps of the Supreme Court to the steps of clinics in every town, from the television and the radio. One might be tempted to think that abortion was a recent phenomenon, invented to incite passion in an otherwise calm political climate.

But abortion is not new. As long as women have found themselves faced with a pregnancy, they have been finding ways to end it. From the ingestion of poisonous herbs and potions mixed and stirred, to the friendly "Cotton-eyed Joe," the blind doctor who never remembered the names or the families of the women he treated, to the back alleys and coat hangers, to *Roe v. Wade,* to RU 486, abortion has been a part of the female condition.

The fact is, abortion exists and will always exist. This collection does not pretend to offer answers or solutions. Nor does it attempt to promote a particular political position. This is not a book about the passion of politics. It is not about politics at all. It is about passion. The passion of women and men who have written about their feelings on abortion.

The works in this collection span almost a century of writing on the subject and sweep across space and time, from the old-world charm of Fyodor Sologub's Russia to the back alleys of Babs H. Deal and Audre Lorde; from the inner dialogue and quiet reserve of the knitter of Amy Hempel's "Beg, Sl Tog, Inc, Cont, Rep," to the sardonic and humorous "1957, a Romance" by Ellen Gilchrist, to the memorable vision of Langston Hughes, whose Cora in "Cora Unashamed" confronts the loss of daughters, both black and white.

This collection offers a diverse and complex take on one of the most talked-about issues of our time. These powerful, thought-provoking works beg, scream, and cry to be heard. They move us past the clichéd public debate and bumper-sticker buzzwords and deep into the hearts and souls of the people who have chosen to write about one of our most publicly debated yet private issues.

COMING TO TERMS

The Abortion

Alice Walker

THEY HAD DISCUSSED IT, BUT NOT DEEPLY, WHETHER they wanted the baby she was now carrying. "I don't *know* if I want it," she said, eyes filling with tears. She cried at anything now, and was often nauseous. That pregnant women cried easily and were nauseous seemed banal to her, and she resented banality.

"Well, think about it," he said, with his smooth reassuring voice (but with an edge of impatience she now felt) that used to soothe her.

It was all she *did* think about, all she apparently *could;* that he could dream otherwise enraged her. But she always lost, when they argued. Her temper would flare up, he would become instantly reasonable, mature, responsible, if not responsive precisely, to her mood, and she would swallow down her tears and hate herself. It was because she believed him "good." The best human being she had ever met.

"It isn't as if we don't already have a child," she said in a calmer tone, carelessly wiping at the tear that slid from one eye.

"We have a perfect child," he said with relish, "thank the Good Lord!"

Had she ever dreamed she'd marry someone humble

enough to go around thanking the Good Lord? She had not.

Now they left the bedroom, where she had been lying down on their massive king-size bed with the forbidding ridge in the middle, and went down the hall—hung with bright prints—to the cheerful, spotlessly clean kitchen. He put water on for tea in a bright yellow pot.

She wanted him to want the baby so much he would try to save its life. On the other hand, she did not permit such presumptuousness. As he praised the child they already had, a daughter of sunny disposition and winning smile, Imani sensed subterfuge, and hardened her heart.

"What am I talking about," she said, as if she'd been talking about it. "Another child would kill me. I can't imagine life with two children. Having a child is a good experience *to have had,* like graduate school. But if you've had one, you've had the experience and that's enough."

He placed the tea before her and rested a heavy hand on her hair. She felt the heat and pressure of his hand as she touched the cup and felt the odor and steam rise up from it. Her throat contracted.

"I can't drink that," she said through gritted teeth. "Take it away."

There were days of this.

Clarice, their daughter, was barely two years old. A miscarriage brought on by grief (Imani had lost her fervidly environmentalist mother to lung cancer shortly after Clarice's birth; the asbestos ceiling in the classroom where she taught first graders had leaked for twenty years) separated Clarice's birth from the new pregnancy. Imani felt her body had been assaulted by these events and was, in fact, considerably weakened, and was also, in any case, chronically anemic and rundown. Still, if she had wanted the baby more than she did not want it, she would not have planned to abort it.

They lived in a small town in the South. Her husband, Clarence, was, among other things, legal adviser and defender of the new black mayor of the town. The mayor was much in their lives because of the difficulties being the first black mayor of a small town assured, and because, next to the major leaders of black struggles in the South, Clarence respected and admired him most.

Imani reserved absolute judgment, but she did point out that Mayor Carswell would never look at her directly when she made a comment or posed a question, even sitting at her own dinner table, and would instead talk to Clarence as if she were not there. He assumed that as a woman she would not be interested in, or even understand, politics. (He would comment occasionally on her cooking or her clothes. He noticed when she cut her hair.) But Imani understood every shade and variation of politics: she understood, for example, why she fed the mouth that did not speak to her; because for the present she must believe in Mayor Carswell, even as he could not believe in her. Even understanding this, however, she found dinners with Carswell hard to swallow.

But Clarence was dedicated to the mayor, and believed his success would ultimately mean security and advancement for them all.

On the morning she left to have the abortion, the mayor and Clarence were to have a working lunch, and they drove her to the airport deep in conversation about municipal funds, racist cops, and the facilities for teaching at the chaotic, newly integrated schools. Clarence had time for the briefest kiss and hug at the airport ramp.

"Take care of yourself," he whispered lovingly as she walked away. He was needed, while she was gone, to draft the city's new charter. She had agreed this was important; the mayor was already being called incompetent by local businessmen and the chamber of commerce, and one inferred from television that no black person alive even knew what a city charter was.

"Take care of myself." Yes, she thought. I see that is what I have to do. But she thought this self-pityingly, which invalidated it. She had expected *him* to take care of her, and she blamed him for not doing so now.

Well, she was a fraud, anyway. She had known after a year of marriage that it bored her. "The Experience of Having a Child" was to distract her from this fact. Still, she expected him to "take care of her." She was lucky he didn't pack up and leave. But he seemed to know, as she did, that if anyone packed and left, it would be her. Precisely *because* she was a fraud and because in the end he would settle for fraud and she could not.

On the plane to New York her teeth ached and she vomited bile—bitter, yellowish stuff she hadn't even been aware her body produced. She resented and appreciated the crisp help of the stewardess, who asked if she needed anything, then stood chatting with the cigarette-smoking white man next to her, whose fat hairy wrist, like a large worm, was all Imani could bear to see out of the corner of her eye.

Her first abortion, when she was still in college, she frequently remembered as wonderful, bearing as it had all the marks of a supreme coming of age and a seizing of the direction of her own life, as well as a comprehension of existence that never left her: that life—what one saw about one and called Life—was not a facade. There was nothing behind it which used "Life" as its manifestation. Life was itself. Period. At the time, and afterward, and even now, this seemed a marvelous thing to know.

The abortionist had been a delightful Italian doctor on the Upper East Side in New York, and before he put her under he told her about his own daughter who was just her age, and a junior at Vassar. He babbled on and on until she was out, but not before Imani had thought how her thousand dollars, for which she would be in debt for years, would go to keep her there.

When she woke up it was all over. She lay on a brown Naugahyde sofa in the doctor's outer office. And she heard, over her somewhere in the air, the sound of a woman's voice. It was a Saturday, no nurses in attendance, and she presumed it was the doctor's wife. She was pulled gently to her feet by this voice and encouraged to walk.

"And when you leave, be sure to walk as if nothing is wrong," the voice said.

Imani did not feel any pain. This surprised her. Perhaps he didn't do anything, she thought. Perhaps he took my thousand dollars and put me to sleep with two dollars' worth of ether. Perhaps this is a racket.

But he was so kind, and he was smiling benignly, almost fatherly, at her (and Imani realized how desperately she needed this "fatherly" look, this "fatherly" smile). "Thank you," she murmured sincerely: she was thanking him for her life.

Some of Italy was still in his voice. "It's nothing, nothing," he said. "A nice, pretty girl like you; in school like my own daughter, you didn't need this trouble."

"He's nice," she said to herself, walking to the subway on her way back to school. She lay down gingerly across a vacant seat, and passed out.

She hemorrhaged steadily for six weeks, and was not well again for a year.

But this was seven years later. An abortion law now made it possible to make an appoinment at a clinic, and for seventy-five dollars a safe, quick, painless abortion was yours.

Imani had once lived in New York, in the Village, not five blocks from where the abortion clinic was. It was also near the Margaret Sanger clinic, where she had received her very first diaphragm, with utter gratitude and amazement that some-one apparently understood and actually cared about young women as alone and ignorant as she. In fact, as she walked up the block, with its modern office buildings side by side with older, more elegant brownstones, she felt how close she was still to that earlier self. Still not in control of her sensuality, and only through violence and with money (for the flight, for the operation itself) in control of her body.

She found that abortion had entered the age of the assembly line. Grateful for the lack of distinction between herself and the other women—all colors, ages, states of misery or ner-vousness—she was less happy to notice, once the doctor started to insert the catheter, that the anesthesia she had been given was insufficient. But assembly lines don't stop because the product on them has a complaint. Her doctor whistled, and assured her she was all right, and carried the procedure through to the horrific end. Imani fainted some seconds before that.

They laid her out in a peaceful room full of cheerful colors. Primary colors: yellow, red, blue. When she revived she had the feeling of being in a nursery. She had a pressing need to urinate.

A nurse, kindly, white-haired and with firm hands, helped her to the toilet. Imani saw herself in the mirror over the sink and was alarmed. She was literally gray, as if all her blood had leaked out.

"Don't worry about how you look," said the nurse. "Rest a bit here and take it easy when you get back home. You'll be fine in a week or so."

She could not imagine being fine again. Somewhere her child—she never dodged into the language of "fetuses" and "amorphous growths"—was being flushed down a sewer. Gone all her or his chances to see the sunlight, savor a fig.

"Well," she said to this child, "it was you or me, kiddo, and I chose me."

There were people who thought she had no right to choose herself, but Imani knew better than to think of those people now.

It was a bright, hot Saturday when she returned.

Clarence and Clarice picked her up at the airport. They had brought flowers from Imani's garden, and Clarice presented them with a stout-hearted hug. Once in her mother's lap she rested content all the way home, sucking her thumb, stroking her nose with the forefinger of the same hand, and kneading a corner of her blanket with the three fingers that were left.

"How did it go?" asked Clarence.

"It went," said Imani.

*

7

There was no way to explain abortion to a man. She thought castration might be an apt analogy, but most men, perhaps all, would insist this could not possibly be true.

"The anesthesia failed," she said. "I thought I'd never faint in time to keep from screaming and leaping off the table."

Clarence paled. He hated the thought of pain, any kind of violence. He could not endure it; it made him physically ill. This was one of the reasons he was a pacifist, another reason she admired him.

She knew he wanted her to stop talking. But she continued in a flat, deliberate voice.

"All the blood seemed to run out of me. The tendons in my legs felt cut. I was gray."

He reached for her hand. Held it. Squeezed.

"But," she said, "at least I know what I don't want. And I intend never to go through any of this again."

They were in the living room of their peaceful, quiet, and colorful house. Imani was in her rocker, Clarice dozing on her lap. Clarence sank to the floor and rested his head against her knees. She felt he was asking for nurture when she needed it herself. She felt the two of them, Clarence and Clarice, clinging to her, using her. And that the only way she could claim herself, feel herself distinct from them, was by doing something painful, self-defining, but self-destructive.

She suffered the pressure of his head as long as she could.

"Have a vasectomy," she said, "or stay in the guest room. Nothing is going to touch me anymore that isn't harmless."

He smoothed her thick hair with his hand. "We'll talk about it," he said, as if that was not what they were doing. "We'll see. Don't worry. We'll take care of things."

She had forgotten that the third Sunday in June, the following day, was the fifth memorial observance for Holly Monroe, who had been shot down on her way home from her high-school graduation ceremony five years before. Imani *always* went to these memorials. She liked the reassurance that her people had long memories, and that those people who fell in struggle or innocence were not forgotten. She was, of course, too weak to go. She was dizzy and still losing blood. The white lawgivers attempted to get around assassination—which Imani considered extreme abortion—by saying the victim provoked it (there had been some difficulty saying this about Holly Monroe, but they had tried) but were antiabortionist to a man. Imani thought of this as she resolutely showered and washed her hair.

Clarence had installed central air conditioning their second year in the house. Imani had at first objected. "I want to smell the trees, the flowers, the natural air!" she cried. But the first summer of 110-degree heat had cured her of giving a damn about any of that. Now she wanted to be cool. As much as she loved trees, on a hot day she would have sawed through a forest to get to an air conditioner.

In fairness to him, she had to admit he asked her if she thought she was well enough to go. But even to be asked annoyed her. She was not one to let her own troubles prevent her from showing proper respect and remembrance toward the dead, although she understood perfectly well that once dead, the dead do not exist. So respect, remembrance was for herself, and today herself needed rest. There was something mad about her refusal to rest, and she felt it as she tottered about getting Clarice dressed. But she did not stop. She ran a bath, plopped the child in it, scrubbed her plump body on her knees, arms straining over the tub awkwardly in a way that made her stomach hurt—but not yet her uterus—dried her hair, lifted her out, and dried the rest of her on the kitchen table.

"You are going to remember as long as you live what kind of people they are," she said to the child, who, gurgling and cooing, looked into her mother's stern face with lighthearted fixation.

"You are going to hear the music," Imani said. "The music they've tried to kill. The music they try to steal." She felt feverish and was aware she was muttering. She didn't care.

"They think they can kill a continent—people, trees, buffalo—and then fly off to the moon and just forget about it. But you and me, we're going to remember the people, the trees, and the fucking buffalo. Goddammit."

"Buffwoe," said the child, hitting at her mother's face with a spoon.

She placed the baby on a blanket in the living room and turned to see her husband's eyes, full of pity, on her. She wore pert green velvet slippers and a lovely sea green robe. Her body was bent within it. A reluctant tear formed beneath his gaze.

"Sometimes I look at you and I wonder, 'What is this man doing in my house?'"

This had started as a joke between them. Her aim had been never to marry, but to take in lovers who could be sent home at dawn, freeing her to work and ramble.

"I'm here because you love me," was the traditional answer. But Clarence faltered, meeting her eyes, and Imani turned away.

It was a hundred degrees by ten o'clock. By eleven, when the memorial service began, it would be ten degrees hotter. Imani staggered from the heat. When she sat in the car, she had to clench her teeth against the dizziness until the motor prodded the air conditioning to envelop them in coolness. A dull ache started in her uterus.

The church was not, of course, air conditioned. It was authentic Primitive Baptist in every sense.

Like the four previous memorials, this one was designed by Holly Monroe's classmates. All twenty-five of whom—fat and thin—managed to look like the dead girl. Imani had never seen Holly Monroe, though there were always photographs of her dominating the pulpit of this church where she had been baptized and where she had sung in the choir—and to her, every black girl of a certain vulnerable age *was* Holly Monroe. And an even deeper truth was that Holly Monroe was herself. Herself shot down, aborted on the eve of becoming herself.

She was prepared to cry and to do so with abandon. But she did not. She clenched her teeth against the steadily increasing pain and her tears were instantly blotted by the heat.

Mayor Carswell had been waiting for Clarence in the vestibule of the church, mopping his plumply jowled faced with a voluminous handkerchief and holding court among half a dozen young men and women who listened to him with awe. Imani exchanged greetings with the mayor, he ritualistically kissed her on the cheek, and kissed Clarice on the cheek, but his rather heat-glazed eye was already fastened on her husband. The two men huddled in a corner away from the awed young group. Away from Imani and Clarice, who passed hesitantly, waiting to be joined or to be called back, into the church.

There was a quarter hour's worth of music.

"Holly Monroe was five feet three inches tall, and weighed one hundred and eleven pounds," her best friend said, not reading from notes, but talking to each person in the audience. "She was a stubborn, loyal Aries, the best kind of friend to have. She had black kinky hair that she experimented with a lot. She was exactly the color of this oak church pew in the summer; in the winter she was the color [pointing up] of this heart pine ceiling. She loved green. She did not like lavender because she said she also didn't like pink. She had brown eyes and wore glasses, except when she was meeting someone for the first time. She had a sort of rounded nose. She had beautiful large teeth, but her lips were always chapped so she didn't smile as much as she might have if she'd ever gotten used to carrying ChapStick. She had elegant feet.

"Her favorite church song was 'Leaning on the Everlasting Arms.' Her favorite other kind of song was 'I Can't Help Myself—I Love You and Nobody Else.' She was often late for choir rehearsal though she loved to sing. She made the dress she wore to her graduation in Home Ec. She *hated* Home Ec...."

Imani was aware that the sound of low, murmurous voices had been the background for this statement all along. Everything was quiet around her, even Clarice sat up straight, absorbed by the simple friendliness of the young woman's voice. All of Holly Monroe's classmates and friends in the choir wore vivid green. Imani imagined Clarice entranced by the brilliant, swaying color as by a field of swaying corn.

Lifting the child, her uterus burning, and perspiration already a stream down her back, Imani tiptoed to the door. Clarence and the mayor were still deep in conversation. She heard "board meeting...aldermen...city council." She beckoned to Clarence.

"Your voices are carrying!" she hissed.

She meant: How dare you not come inside.

They did not. Clarence raised his head, looked at her, and shrugged his shoulders helplessly. Then, turning, with the abstracted air of priests, the two men moved slowly toward the outer door, and into the churchyard, coming to stand some distance from the church beneath a large oak tree. There they remained throughout the service.

Two years later, Clarence was furious with her: What is the matter with you? he asked. You never want me to touch you. You told me to sleep in the guest room and I did. You told me to have a vasectomy I didn't want and *I did*. (Here, there was a sob of hatred for her somewhere in the anger, the humiliation: he thought of himself as a eunuch, and blamed her.)

She was not merely frigid, she was remote.

She had been amazed after they left the church that the anger she'd felt watching Clarence and the mayor turn away from the Holly Monroe memorial did not prevent her accepting a ride home with him. A month later it did not prevent her smiling on him fondly. Did not prevent a trip to Bermuda, a few blissful days of very good sex on a deserted beach screened by trees. Did not prevent her listening to his mother's stories of Clarence's youth as though she would treasure them forever.

And yet. From that moment in the heat at the church door, she had uncoupled herself from him, in a separation that made him, except occasionally, little more than a stranger.

And he had not felt it, had not known.

"What have I done?" he asked, all the tenderness in his voice breaking over her. She smiled a nervous smile at him, which he interpreted as derision—so far apart had they drifted.

They had discussed the episode at the church many times.

Mayor Carswell—whom they never saw anymore—was now a model mayor, with wide biracial support in his campaign for the legislature. Neither could easily recall him, though television frequently brought him into the house.

"It was so important that I help the mayor!" said Clarence. "He was our *first!*"

Imani understood this perfectly well, but it sounded humorous to her. When she smiled, he was offended.

She had known the moment she left the marriage, the exact second. But apparently that moment had left no perceptible mark.

They argued, she smiled, they scowled, blamed and cried—as she packed.

Each of them almost recalled out loud that about this time of the year their aborted child would have been a troublesome, "terrible" two-year-old, a great burden on its mother, whose health was by now in excellent shape, each wanted to think aloud that the marriage would have deteriorated anyway, because of that.

From
Play It As It Lays
Joan Didion

THE FLOOR OF THE BEDROOM WHERE IT HAPPENED
was covered with newspapers. She remembered reading
somewhere that newspapers were antiseptic, it had to do with
the chemicals in the ink, to deliver a baby in a farmhouse you
covered the floor with newspapers. There was something else
to be done with newspapers, something unexpected, some
emergency trick: quilts could be made with newspapers. In
time of disaster you could baste newspapers to both sides of a
cotton blanket and end up with a warm quilt. She knew a lot
of things about disaster. She could manage. Carter could
never manage but she could. She could not think where she
had learned all these tricks. Probably in her mother's *American
Red Cross Handbook,* gray with a red cross on the cover. There,
that was a good thing to think about, at any rate not a bad
thing if she kept her father out of it. If she could concentrate
for even one minute on a picture of herself as a ten-year-old
sitting on the front steps of the house in Silver Wells reading
the gray book with the red cross on the cover (splints, shock,
rattlesnake bite, rattlesnake bite was why her mother made
her read it) with the heat shimmering off the corrugated tin
roof of the shed across the road (her father was not in this pic-

ture, keep him out of it, say he had gone into Vegas with Benny Austin), if she could concentrate for one more minute on that shed, on whether this minute twenty years later the heat still shimmered off its roof, those were two minutes during which she was not entirely party to what was happening in this bedroom in Encino.

Two minutes in Silver Wells, two minutes here, two minutes there, it was going to be over in this bedroom in Encino, it could not last forever. The walls of the bedroom were cream-colored, yellow, a wallpaper with a modest pattern. Whoever had chosen that wallpaper would have liked maple furniture, a maple bedroom set, a white chenille bedspread and a white Princess telephone, all gone now but she could see it as it must have been, could see even the woman who had picked the wallpaper, she would be a purchaser of Audubon prints and scented douches, a hoarder of secret sexual grievances, a wife. Two minutes in Silver Wells, two minutes on the wallpaper, it could not last forever. The table was a doctor's table but not fitted with stirrups: instead there were two hardbacked chairs with pillows tied over the backs. "Tell me if it's too cold," the doctor said. The doctor was tall and haggard and wore a rubber apron. "Tell me now because I won't be able to touch the air conditioner once I start."

She said that it was not too cold.

"No, it's too cold. You don't weigh enough, it's too cold."

He adjusted the dial but the sound remained level. She closed her eyes and tried to concentrate on the sound. Carter did not like air conditioners but there had been one somewhere. She had slept in a room with an air conditioner, the question was where, never mind the question, that question led nowhere. "This is just induced menstruation," she could

hear the doctor saying. "Nothing to have any emotional difficulties about, better not to think about it at all, quite often the
pain is worse when we think about it, don't like anesthetics,
anesthetics are where we run into trouble, just a little local on
the cervix, there, relax, Maria, I said *relax*."

No moment more or less important than any other
moment, all the same: the pain as the doctor scraped signified
nothing beyond itself, no more constituted the patter of her
life than did the movie on television in the living room of this
house in Encino. The man in the white duck pants was sitting
out there watching the movie and she was lying in here not
watching the movie, and that was all there was to that. Why
the volume on the set was turned up so high seemed another
question better left unasked. "Hear that scraping, Maria?"
the doctor said. "That should be the sound of music to
you...don't scream, Maria, there are people next door, almost
done, almost over, better to get it all now than do it again a
month from now...I said don't make any noise, Maria, now
I'll tell you what's going to happen, you'll bleed a day or so, not
heavily, just spotting, and then a month, six weeks from now
you'll have a normal period, not this month, this month you
just had it, it's in that pail."

He went into the bathroom then (later she would try to fix
in her mind the exact circumstances of his leaving the bedroom, would try to remember if he took the pail with him,
later that would seem important to her) and by the time he
came back the contractions had stopped. He gave her one
envelope of tetracycline capsules and another of ergot tablets
and by six o'clock of that hot October afternoon she was out of
the bedroom in Encino and back in the car with the man in
the white duck pants. The late sun seemed warm and benevo-

lent on her skin and everything she saw looked beautiful, the summer pulse of life itself made manifest. As she backed out of the driveway she smiled radiantly at her companion.

"You missed a pretty fair movie," he said. "Paula Raymond." He reached into his pocket for what seemed to be a cigarette holder. "Ever since I gave up smoking I carry these by the dozen, they look like regular holders but all you get is air."

Maria stared at his outstretched hand.

"*Take* it. I noticed you're still smoking. You'll thank me some day."

"Thank you."

"I'm a regular missionary." The man in the white duck pants resettled his soft bulk and gazed out the car window. "Gee, Paula Raymond was a pretty girl," he said then. "Funny she never became a star."

The Kiss of the Unborn

Fyodor Sologub

I

IN THE OFFICE OF A LARGE BUSINESS FIRM, A BRIGHT
young boy with close-cropped hair and two rows of tiny brass
buttons on his tight jacket—it was dusty but didn't show it
because it was gray—glanced through the door of the room
where the five typists were at work, pounding away simulta-
neously on five noisily rattling machines, and taking hold of
the lintel and swinging on one foot, he said to one of the girls:

"Nadezhda Alekseevna, Mrs. Kolymtseva wants you on the
phone."

He ran off and his steps were inaudible on the gray mat
extending down the narrow corridor. Nadezhda Alekseevna,
a tall, shapely girl of about twenty-seven, with confident,
quiet movements and with that profound look of tranquillity
which is given only to those who have experienced difficult
days, finished typing to the end of the line, stood up and
unhurriedly walked downstairs to the room by the entry
where the telephone was. She was thinking:

"What's happened now?"

She was now used to the fact that if her sister Tatyana Alekseevna wrote to her or phoned her, it was almost always
because something had happened in the family: the children

were sick, there was something unpleasant at her husband's work, some event in the school where the children went, or an acute attack of money troubles. Then Nadezhda Alekseevna would take a streetcar and set off for the outlying district of the city—to help, to console, to come to the rescue. Her sister was some ten years older than Nadezhda Alekseevna, she had been married for a long time; and although they lived in the same city, they did not see one another often.

In the cramped telephone booth, where for some reason it always smelled of tobacco, beer, and mice, Nadezhda Alekseevna took the receiver and said:

"Hello. Is it you, Tanichka?"

She heard her sister's voice, tear-filled and agitated, just exactly as Nadezhda Alekseevna had expected it to be:

"Nadya, for God's sake, come right away. We've had a horrible misfortune, Seryozha is dead, he shot himself."

Not having had time to be frightened by this unexpected news about the death of her fifteen-year-old nephew Seryozha, Nadezhda Alekseevna somewhat confusedly and disjointedly said:

"Tanya, dear, what are you saying! How horrible! But why? When did it happen?"

And, neither expecting nor listening to the answer, she said hurriedly:

"I'll come right away, right away."

She threw down the receiver, even forgetting to put it on the hook, and quickly went to the supervisor to ask for leave due to family circumstances.

The supervisor allowed her to leave, although he made a dissatisfied face and growled:

"You know it's a very busy time before the holidays. All of

you always have something urgent happening at the most inopportune time for us. Well, okay, go on if you have to, but just remember that the work's piling up."

II

Several minutes later, Nadezhda Alekseevna was already on the streetcar. She had to travel about twenty minutes. During that time, Nadezhda Alekseevna's thoughts turned again in that direction they always took at those moments in life, when life's all-too-frequent surprises, almost always unpleasant, destroyed the tedious flow of the days. But Nadezhda Alekseevna's feelings were vague and suppressed. Only from time to time the deep pity for her sister and for the boy suddenly caused her heart to contract painfully.

It was terrifying to think that this fifteen-year-old boy, who just the other day had come to Nadezhda Alekseevna and talked with her for a long time, this formerly cheerful schoolboy Seryozha had suddenly shot himself. It was painful to think about how his mother would grieve and weep—she, who without this, was already wearied by a difficult and not very successful life. But perhaps there was something else more difficult and terrifying hanging over her life, that prevented Nadezhda Alekseevna from giving herself up to these feelings—and her heart, crowded with long-standing sorrow, was incapable of being sweetly exhausted by the torments of grief, pity, and terror. It was as if the source of assuaging tears was weighed down by a heavy stone—and only meager, occasional little tears welled up sometimes in her eyes whose usual expression was one of indifferent boredom.

Again her memory took Nadezhda Alekseevna back to that same passionate, flaming circle through which she had passed. She was remembering several years before, when she had lived those few days of self-oblivion and passion, of love, given without measure.

The bright summer days were like a holiday for Nadezhda Alekseevna. The heavens turned a joyful blue for her, above the wretched expanses of the Finnish countryside, and the summer rainshowers made amusing, happy noises. The odor of resin in the warm pine forest was more sweetly intoxicating than the fragrance of roses, which did not grow in that region that was so gloomy, but still gladdened the heart. The greenish-gray moss in the dark forest was like a sweet bed of bliss. The forest brook, streaming among the gray, awkwardly scattered stones, murmured so joyfully and sonorously, as if its transparent water were rushing straight for the fields of happy Arcady; and the coolness of those sonorous streams was delightful and joyful.

The happy days raced by so quickly for Nadezhda Alekseevna in the delightful ecstasy of being in love, and the final day came, but of course she did not know it was to be the final happy day. As always, everything about was cloudless and bright and artlessly delightful. As always, the vast shadow of the forest was cool and pensive, redolent with resin, and as always, the warm moss was joyfully tender underfoot. Only the birds had already ceased to sing—they had built their nests and were raising their young.

But there was a vague shadow on her beloved's face. It was because he had received an unpleasant letter that morning.

As he said himself:

"It's a terribly unpleasant letter. I am desperate. I won't be able to see you for several days!"

"Why?" she asked.

And she still had no time to be sad. But he said:

"My father writes that mother is ill. I have to leave."

His father had written something quite different, but Nadezhda Alekseevna did not know about that. She still did not know that love can be deceived, that lips which have kissed, can tell a lie as well as the truth.

He said, embracing and kissing Nadezhda Alekseevna:

"There's nothing I can do; I have to go! What a bore! I'm sure it's nothing serious, but still I can't not go."

"Yes, of course," she said, "if your mother is sick, then you must go! But write to me every day. I'll miss you so!"

She accompanied him, as always, to the large road at the edge of the forest, and then she walked home along the forest path, somewhat saddened, but convinced that he would soon return. But he did not return.

Nadezhda Alekseevna received several letters from him—they were strange letters. There was a touch of embarrassment in them, a sense of reticence, some kind of incomprehensible hints that frightened one. And these letters came less and less often. Nadezhda Alekseevna grew to suspect that he had ceased to love her. And suddenly she learned from strangers, in a chance conversation at the end of that summer, that he was already married.

"How is it that you didn't hear? Last week, right after the wedding, they took off for Nice."

"Yes, he's a lucky one—he caught a rich and beautiful wife."

"She had a big dowry?"

"I'll say! Her father...."

She had already ceased listening to what the father had. She walked away.

She often thought back on everything that had happened afterward. She didn't want to remember—Nadezhda Alekseevna tried to drive away those memories, to stifle them in herself. It had been so difficult and demeaning, and so unavoidable then, during those first difficult days after she had learned about his marriage—and having sensed herself to be a mother there, among those dear places where she was still reminded of his caresses—having just felt the first movements of a new being, to be thinking already of its death. And to kill the unborn!

No one from home found out; Nadezhda Alekseevna thought up a plausible pretext for being away from home for two weeks. Somehow, with great difficulty, she got together the money needed to pay for a wicked deed. It was in some vile refuge that they had performed the terrible deed, the details of which she did not want to remember later, and she returned home, still half-sick, emaciated, pale, and weak, a pitiful heroism covering up her pain and terror.

Recollections about the details of this deed were persistent, but still Nadezhda Alekseevna was able somehow to deny them lasting power over her memory. She would recall everything quickly, hastily, then shudder from terror and loathing—and hasten to distract herself from those pictures with something.

But what was persistent, and what Nadezhda Alekseevna could not and did not want to struggle with, was the dear and terrifying image of the unborn one, her child.

When Nadezhda Alekseevna was alone and sitting calmly with her eyes closed, a small child would come to her. It seemed to her that she could see how he was growing up. So lifelike were these sensations, that at times it seemed to her as if she were experiencing, year after year, day after day, all that a true mother of a living child does. At times it seemed to her that her breasts were full of milk. Later she shuddered when she heard the noise of some falling object—perhaps her child had hurt itself.

Sometimes Nadezhda Alekseevna wanted to have a talk with him, take him in her arms and caress him. She held out a hand to smooth the soft, golden-light hair of her son, but her hand met emptiness and she imagined that behind her back she heard the laughter of her child who had run off and hidden somewhere nearby.

She knew his face—it was her own child, even if he had not been born. She saw his face clearly—the dear and terrible combinations of her features with those of the one who had taken her love and discarded it, who had taken her soul and drained it and then forgotten it—his features, which in spite of everything, remained dear.

His happy, gray eyes are from his father. The fine little shells of his pink ears are from his mother. The soft outline of his lips and his chin are his father's. The rounded, delicate shoulders, similar to the shoulders of a young girl, are from his mother. The golden, slightly wavy hair is from his father. The endearing dimples on his rosy cheeks are from his mother.

Thus Nadezhda Alekseevna sorts out everything, both the little hands and feet, and recognizes everything. She knows everything. She recognizes his habits—how he holds his hands, how he crosses one leg over the other—he took this from his father, even though the unborn one had not seen his own father. He begins to laugh and looks askance, blushing tenderly and bashfully—this is from his mother, the unborn one took this from his mother.

It is sweet and painful. It is as if someone cruel and dear opened up a deep wound with a tender, pink little finger—it is so painful! But it is impossible to banish him.

"And I don't want to, I don't want to banish you, my unborn child. At least live, as you are able to. At least I will give you this life."

Only a life in dreams. He only exists in her. My dear, poor unborn one! You yourself do not rejoice, you yourself do not laugh for yourself, you yourself do not cry for yourself. You live, but there is no you. In the world of the living, among people and objects, there is no you. So alive, and dear, and bright—and there is no you.

"Oh what have I done with you!"

And Nadezhda Alekseevna was thinking:

"He's still little and doesn't know. When he grows up, he'll find out and compare himself with those who have been born, and he'll want a living life and he'll reproach his mother. Then I shall die."

She neither noticed nor considered that her thoughts would seem mad if they were to be judged by common sense, by that terrible and mad judge of our deeds. She did not consider that that small, unformed, wrinkled fetus which she had discarded, remained just that—an inanimate lump of matter, a dead substance to which the human spirit had not given animate form. No, for Nadezhda Alekseevna, her unborn one was alive and her heart suffered unending torment.

He was all light, in light clothes with little white hands and feet, clear, innocent eyes, a pure smile, and when he laughed, he laughed joyfully and sonorously. True, when she wanted to embrace him, he ran off and hid, but he did not run far away and he hid somewhere nearby. He ran off from her embraces, but on the other hand, he himself often threw his warm tender little arms around her neck, and pressed his delicate lips to her cheek—during those minutes when she was sitting quietly with her eyes closed. Only he never once kissed her directly on the lips.

"He will grow up and understand," thought Nadezhda Alekseevna, "he will grieve, turn away, leave forever. Then I shall die."

And now, sitting in the monotonously rumbling cramped streetcar, among bundled-up strangers with their holiday purchases in their laps, Nadezhda Alekseevna closed her eyes and once more saw her child. Once more she looked into his clear eyes, heard his light prattling—she was not paying attention to the words—and in this way she rode to the place where she had to get off.

III

Nadezhda Alekseevna stepped out of the streetcar and walked along the snowy streets past the low stone and wooden houses, past the gardens and fences of this distant suburb. She was walking alone. She ran into strangers—her dear and terrifying one was not with Nadezhda Alekseevna. And she was thinking:

"My sin is always with me and there is nowhere for me to go to escape it. Why then do I live? And here Seryozha has died."

She walked and there was a dull grief in her heart and she did not know how to answer this question for herself.

"Why am I living? But why should I die?"

And she was thinking:

"He is always with me, my little one. He is already growing up, he is eight years old and he must understand a great deal. Why then does he not get angry at me? Doesn't he really want to play with the little children here about, go sledding on the icy slopes? All the charm of our earthly life, everything that even I enjoyed so brightly, all of this charm, this perhaps deceptive, but so entrancing charm of life on this dear earth, in this best of all possible worlds, doesn't it entice him?"

Now, while Nadezhda Alekseevna was walking alone, along the strange, indifferent street, her thoughts did not remain long on herself and her child. She remembered her sister's family, where she was going: her sister's husband, overloaded with work, her sister who was always tired, the horde of little children, noisy, capricious, eternally demanding one thing or another, the wretched apartment, the lack of money. Her nephews and nieces whom Nadezhda Alekseevna loved. And the schoolboy who had shot himself, Seryozha.

Could one have expected this? He had been such a happy, smart boy.

But then Nadezhda Alekseevna remembered a conversation with Seryozha from last week. The boy had been sad and agitated. They were talking about something they had read in the Russian newspapers, no doubt something nightmarish. Seryozha was saying:

"It's awful at home and then you take the newspaper and all you see is terror and filth."

Nadezhda Alekseevna answered something which she herself didn't believe, only in order to distract the boy from his distressing thoughts. Seryozha smiled somberly and said:

"Aunt Nadya, just think how bad all of this is! Just think what's going on around us! Isn't it really terrifying if the best of men, and so old, flees his own house and dies somewhere! He only saw more clearly than any of us that terror in which we all live and he couldn't bear it. He left and died. It's terrifying!"

Then, after a period of silence, Seryozha spoke the words which had frightened Nadezhda Alekseevna at the time:

"Aunt Nadya, I'll tell you frankly because you are a dear and you'll understand me—I don't want at all to live in the middle of all that's going on now. I know that I'm just as weak as everyone else, but what can I do? I'll just be drawn into this vileness, bit by bit. Aunt Nadya, Nekrasov was right: 'It is good to die young.'"

Nadezhda Alekseevna was very frightened and talked with Seryozha for a long time. Finally, it seemed to her that he believed her. He smiled happily as he used to smile and said, in his former carefree tone:

"Okay. We'll live and we'll see. 'Progress advances and where it will end no one knows.'"

Seryozha loved to read, not Nadson and not Balmont, but Nekrasov.

And now there is no Seryozha, he shot himself. So he did not want to live and observe the majestic procession of progress. What is his mother doing now? Kissing his hands which have become waxen? Or is she smearing butter on bread for the little ones who have gone hungry since morning, frightened and tear-stained, so pitiful in their tattered little dresses and in their jackets with worn-out elbows? Or is she simply lying on the bed and crying, endlessly crying? She is fortunate, fortunate if she can cry! What in the world is sweeter than tears?

IV

Finally, Nadezhda Alekseevna reached their house, climbed to the fifth floor, up the narrow stone stairway with its steep steps; she climbed quickly, almost ran, so that she was panting, and before ringing, she stopped to catch her breath. She was breathing heavily and she held on to the narrow iron strip of railing with her right hand in its warm, knitted glove and looked at the door.

The door was upholstered with felt and covered with oilcloth and this oilcloth was crisscrossed with narrow black stripes for decoration or strengthening. One of these stripes was torn in two and was hanging down, the oilcloth in this place was torn, and the gray felt protruded. And because of this, Nadezhda Alekseevna was suddenly sorry and pained for some reason. Her shoulders began to shake. She quickly covered her face with her hands and began to cry loudly. It was as if she had suddenly become weak; she quickly sat down on the top step, and cried for a long time, with her face covered. Abundant tears flowed from her closed eyes over the warm, knitted gloves.

It was cold, quiet, half-dark on the stairway, and the tightly closed doors—three on one landing—were unmoving and mute. Nadezhda Alekseevna cried for a long time. Suddenly she heard the familiar, light steps. She froze in joyful anticipation. And he, her little one, embraced her neck and again clung to her cheek, moving aside with his little warm hand her hand in the knitted glove. He clung with his tender lips and said to her quietly:

"Why are you crying? You're not guilty!"

She was silent, and listened and did not dare to move and open her eyes for fear he might leave. Only her right hand, the one that he had moved aside, she let drop on her lap; and she covered her eyes with her left hand. And she tried to hold back her tears so as not to frighten him with her unattractive womanly weeping, the weeping of a wretched, earthly woman.

And he said to her again:

"You're not guilty of anything."

And again he began to kiss her cheek. And he said to her, repeating Seryozha's terrifying words:

"I don't want to live here. I thank you, dear mama."

And again he said:

"It's true, believe me, dear mama. I don't want to live."

These words which were so terrifying when Seryozha had said them, were terrifying because the one who said them had received the living form of a human being from a mysterious power and he should have preserved the treasure given to him and not destroyed it: now these same words, in the mouth of the unborn, were joyful for his mother. Ever so quietly, afraid to frighten him with the coarse sound of earthly words, she asked:

"Dear one, have you forgiven me?"

And he answered:

"You aren't guilty of anything. But if you wish, I forgive you."

And suddenly Nadezhda Alekseevna's heart was filled with a foreboding of unexpected joy. Still not daring to hope, still not knowing what would happen, slowly and timidly she extended her hands—and on her lap she felt him, her unborn one, and his hands lay on her shoulders and his lips pressed to her lips. She kissed him for a long while and it seemed to her that the bright eyes of her unborn one, bright as the sun of a benevolent world, looked directly into her eyes, but she dared not open them for fear she would die, having seen that which is forbidden man to see.

When the child relaxed his embrace, and the light footsteps were heard on the stairs, and her child had left, Nadezhda Alekseevna stood up, wiped away her tears, and rang the bell to her sister's apartment. She went to them, calm and happy, to give help to those exhausted from sadness.

Cora Unashamed

Langston Hughes

I

MELTON WAS ONE OF THOSE MISERABLE IN-BETWEEN little places, not large enough to be a town, nor small enough to be a village—that is, a village in the rural, charming sense of the word. Melton had no charm about it. It was merely a nondescript collection of houses and buildings in a region of farms—one of those sad American places with sidewalks, but no paved streets; electric lights, but no sewage; a station, but no trains that stopped, save a jerky local, morning and evening. And it was 150 miles from any city at all—even Sioux City.

Cora Jenkins was one of the least of the citizens of Melton. She was what the people referred to when they wanted to be polite, as a Negress, and when they wanted to be rude, as a nigger—sometimes adding the word "wench" for no good reason, for Cora was usually an inoffensive soul, except that she sometimes cussed.

She had been in Melton for forty years. Born there. Would die there probably. She worked for the Studevants, who treated her like a dog. She stood it. Had to stand it; or work for poorer white folks who would treat her worse; or go jobless. Cora was like a tree—once rooted, she stood, in spite of storms and strife, wind, and rocks, in the earth.

She was the Studevants' maid of all work—washing, iron-ing, cooking, scrubbing, taking care of kids, nursing old folks, making fires, carrying water.

Cora, bake three cakes for Mary's birthday tomorrow night. You Cora, give Rover a bath in that tar soap I bought. Cora, take Ma some jello, and don't let her have even a taste of that raisin pie. She'll keep us up all night if you do. Cora, iron my stockings. Cora, come here…Cora, put…Cora…Cora… Cora! Cora!

And Cora would answer, "Yes, m'am."

The Studevants thought they owned her, and they were probably right: they did. There was something about the teeth in the trap of economic circumstance that kept her in their power practically all her life—in the Studevant kitchen, cooking; in the Studevant parlor, sweeping; in the Studevant backyard, hanging clothes.

You want to know how that could be? How a trap could close so tightly? Here is the outline:

Cora was the oldest of a family of eight children—the Jenk-ins niggers. The only Negroes in Melton, thank God! Where they came from originally—that is, the old folks—God knows. The kids were born there. The old folks are still there now: Pa drives a junk wagon. The old woman ails around the house, ails and quarrels. Seven kids are gone. Only Cora remains. Cora simply couldn't go, with nobody else to help take care of Ma. And before that she couldn't go, with nobody to see that her brothers and sisters got through school (she the oldest, and Ma ailing). And before that—well, somebody had to help Ma look after one baby behind another that kept on coming.

As a child Cora had no playtime. She always had a little brother, or a little sister in her arms. Bad, crying, bratty babies, hungry and mean. In the eighth grade she quit school and went to work with the Studevants.

After that, she ate better. Half day's work at first, helping Ma at home the rest of the time. Then full days, bringing home her pay to feed her father's children. The old man was rather a drunkard. What little money he made from closet-cleaning, ash-hauling, and junk-dealing he spent mostly on the stuff that makes you forget you have eight kids.

He passed the evenings telling long, comical lies to the white riff-raff of the town, and drinking licker. When his horse died, Cora's money went for a new one to haul her Pa and his rickety wagon around. When the mortgage money came due, Cora's wages kept the man from taking the roof from over their heads. When Pa got in jail, Cora borrowed ten dollars from Mrs. Studevant and got him out.

Cora stinted, and Cora saved, and wore the Studevants' old clothes, and ate the Studevants' leftover food, and brought her pay home. Brothers and sisters grew up. The boys, lonesome, went away, as far as they could from Melton. One by one, the girls left too, mostly in disgrace. "Ruinin' ma name," Pa Jenkins said, "Ruinin' ma good name! They can't go out berryin' but what they come back in disgrace." There was something about the cream-and-tan Jenkins girls that attracted the white farm hands.

Even Cora, the humble, had a lover once. He came to town on a freight train (long ago now), and worked at the livery-stable. (That was before autos got to be so common.) Everybody said he was an I.W.W. Cora didn't care. He was the first man and the last she ever remembered wanting. She had never known a colored lover. There weren't any around. That was not her fault.

This white boy, Joe, he always smelt like the horses. He was some kind of foreigner. Had an accent, and yellow hair, big hands, and grey eyes.

It was summer. A few blocks beyond the Studevants' house, meadows and orchards and sweet fields stretched away to the far horizon. At night, stars in the velvet sky. Moon sometimes. Crickets and katydids and lightning bugs. The scent of grass. Cora waiting. That boy, Joe, a cigarette spark far off, whistling in the dark. Love didn't take long—Cora with the scent of the Studevants' supper about her, and a cheap perfume. Joe, big and strong and careless as the horses he took care of, smelling like the stable.

Ma would quarrel because Cora came home late, or because none of the kids had written for three or four weeks, or because Pa was drunk again. Thus the summer passed, a dream of big hands and grey eyes.

Cora didn't go anywhere to have her child. Nor tried to hide it. When the baby grew big within her, she didn't feel that it was a disgrace. The Studevants told her to go home and stay there. Joe left town. Pa cussed. Ma cried. One April morning the kid was born. She had grey eyes, and Cora called her Josephine, after Joe.

Cora was humble and shameless before the fact of the child. There were no Negroes in Melton to gossip, and she didn't care what the white people said. They were in another world. Of course, she hadn't expected to marry Joe, or keep him. He was of that other world, too. But the child was hers—a living bridge between two worlds. Let people talk.

Cora went back to work at the Studevants'—coming home at night to nurse her kid, and quarrel with Ma. About that time, Mrs. Art Studevant had a child, too, and Cora nursed it.

The Studevants' little girl was named Jessie. As the two children began to walk and talk, Cora sometimes brought Josephine to play with Jessie—until the Studevants objected, saying she could get her work done better if she left her child at home.

"Yes, m'am," said Cora.

But in a little while they didn't need to tell Cora to leave her child at home, for Josephine died of whooping-cough. One rosy afternoon, Cora saw the little body go down into the ground in a white casket that cost four weeks' wages.

Since Ma was ailing, Pa, smelling of licker, stood with her at the grave. The two of them alone. Cora was not humble before the fact of death. As she turned away from the hole, tears came—but at the same time a stream of curses so violent that they made the grave-tenders look up in startled horror.

She cussed out God for taking away the life that she herself had given. She screamed, "My baby! God damn it! My baby! I bear her and you take her away!" She looked at the sky where the sun was setting and yelled in defiance. Pa was amazed and scared. He pulled her up on his rickety wagon and drove off, clattering down the road between green fields and sweet meadows that stretched away to the far horizon. All through the ugly town Cora wept and cursed, using all the bad words she had learned from Pa in his drunkenness.

The next week she went back to the Studevants. She was gentle and humble in the face of life—she loved their baby. In the afternoons on the back porch, she would pick little Jessie up and rock her to sleep, burying her dark face in the milky smell of the white child's hair.

II

The years passed. Pa and Ma Jenkins only dried up a little. Old Man Studevant died. The old lady had two strokes. Mrs. Art Studevant and her husband began to look their age, greying hair and sagging stomachs. The children were grown, or nearly so. Kenneth took over the management of the hardware store that Grandpa had left. Jack went off to college. Mary was a teacher. Only Jessie remained a child—her last year in high school. Jessie, nineteen now, and rather slow in her studies, graduating at last. In the Fall she would go to Normal.

Cora hated to think about her going away. In her heart she had adopted Jessie. In that big and careless household it was always Cora who stood like a calm and sheltering tree for Jessie to run to in her troubles. As a child, when Mrs. Art spanked her, as soon as she could, the tears still streaming, Jessie would find her way to the kitchen and Cora. At each school term's end, when Jessie had usually failed in some of her subjects (she quite often failed, being a dull child), it was Cora who saw the report card first with the bad marks on it. Then Cora would devise some way of breaking the news gently to the old folks.

Her mother was always a little ashamed of stupid Jessie, for Mrs. Art was the civic and social leader of Melton, president of the Woman's Club three years straight, and one of the pillars of her church. Mary, the elder, the teacher, would follow with dignity in her footsteps, but Jessie! That child! Spankings in her youth, and scoldings now, did nothing to Jessie's inner being. She remained a plump, dull, freckled girl, placid and strange. Everybody found fault with her but Cora.

In the kitchen Jessie bloomed. She laughed. She talked. She was sometimes even witty. And she learned to cook wonder-

fully. With Cora, everything seemed so simple—not hard and
involved like algebra, or Latin grammar, or the civic problems
of Mama's club, or the sermons at the church. Nowhere in
Melton, nor with anyone, did Jessie feel so comfortable as with
Cora in the kitchen. She knew her mother looked down on
her as a stupid girl. And with her father there was no bond.
He was always too busy buying and selling to bother with the
kids. And often he was off in the city. Old doddering
Grandma made Jessie sleepy and sick. Cousin Nora (Mother's
cousin) was as stiff and prim as a minister's daughter. And
Jessie's older brothers and sister went their ways, seeing Jessie
hardly at all, except at the big table at mealtimes.

Like all the unpleasant things in the house, Jessie was left to
Cora. And Cora was happy. To have a child to raise, a child the
same age as her Josephine would have been, gave her a purpose in life, a warmth inside herself. It was Cora who nursed
and mothered and petted and loved the dull little Jessie
through the years. And now Jessie was a young woman, graduating (late) from high school.

But something had happened to Jessie. Cora knew it before
Mrs. Art did. Jessie was not too stupid to have a boyfriend. She
told Cora about it like a mother. She was afraid to tell Mrs.
Art. Afraid! Afraid! Afraid!

Cora said, "I'll tell her." So, humble and unashamed about
life, one afternoon she marched into Mrs. Art's sun porch and
announced quite simply, "Jessie's going to have a baby."

Cora smiled, but Mrs. Art stiffened like a bolt. Her mouth went
dry. She rose like a soldier. Sat down. Rose again. Walked straight
toward the door, turned around, and whispered, "What?"

"Yes, m'am, a baby. She told me. A little child. Its father is
Willie Matsoulos, whose folks runs the ice-cream stand on

Main. She told me. They want to get married, but Willie ain't here now. He don't know yet about the child."

Cora would have gone on humbly and shamelessly talking about the little unborn had not Mrs. Art fallen into uncontrollable hysterics. Cousin Nora came running from the library, her glasses on a chain. Old Lady Studevant's wheel-chair rolled up, doddering and shaking with excitement. Jessie came, when called, red and sweating, but had to go out, for when her mother looked up from the couch and saw her she yelled louder than ever. There was a rush for camphor bottles and water and ice. Crying and praying followed all over the house. Scandalization! Oh, my Lord! Jessie was in trouble.

"She ain't in trouble neither," Cora insisted. "No trouble having a baby you want. I had one."

"Shut up, Cora!"

"Yes, m'am....But I had one."

"Hush, I tell you."

"Yes, m'am."

III

Then it was that Cora began to be shut out. Jessie was confined to her room. That afternoon, when Miss Mary came home from school, the four white women got together behind closed doors in Mrs. Art's bedroom. For once Cora cooked supper in the kitchen without being bothered by an interfering voice. Mr. Studevant was away in Des Moines. Somehow Cora wished he was home. Big and gruff as he was, he had more sense than the women. He'd probably make a shotgun wedding out of it. But left to Mrs. Art, Jessie would never marry the Greek boy at all. This Cora knew. No man had been found yet good enough for sister Mary to mate with.

Mrs. Art had ambitions which didn't include the likes of Greek ice-cream makers' sons.

Jessie was crying when Cora brought her supper up. The black woman sat down on the bed and lifted the white girl's head in her dark hands. "Don't you mind, honey," Cora said. "Just sit tight, and when the boy comes back I'll tell him how things are. If he loves you he'll want you. And there ain't no reason why you can't marry, neither—you both white. Even if he is a foreigner, he's a right nice boy."

"He loves me," Jessie said. "I know he does. He said so."

But before the boy came back (or Mr. Studevant either) Mrs. Art and Jessie went to Kansas City. "For an Easter shopping trip," the weekly paper said.

Then Spring came in full bloom, and the fields and orchards at the edge of Melton stretched green and beautiful to the far horizon. Cora remembered her own Spring, twenty years ago, and a great sympathy and pain welled up in her heart for Jessie, who was the same age that Josephine would have been, had she lived. Sitting on the kitchen porch shelling peas, Cora thought back over her own life—years and years of working for the Studevants; years and years of going home to nobody but Ma and Pa; little Josephine dead; only Jessie to keep her heart warm. And she knew that Jessie was the dearest thing she had in the world. All the time the girl was gone now, she worried.

After ten days, Mrs. Art and her daughter came back. But Jessie was thinner and paler than she'd ever been in her life. There was no light in her eyes at all. Mrs. Art looked a little scared as they got off the train.

"She had an awful attack of indigestion in Kansas City," she told the neighbors and club women. "That's why I stayed away so long, waiting for her to be able to travel. Poor Jessie! She looks healthy, but she's never been a strong child. She's one of the worries of my life." Mrs. Art talked a lot, explained a lot, about how Jessie had eaten the wrong things in Kansas City.

At home, Jessie went to bed. She wouldn't eat. When Cora brought her food up, she whispered, "The baby's gone."

Cora's face went dark. She bit her lips to keep from cursing. She put her arms about Jessie's neck. The girl cried. Her food went untouched.

A week passed. They tried to *make* Jessie eat then. But the food wouldn't stay in her stomach. Her eyes grew yellow, her tongue white, her heart acted crazy. They called in old Doctor Brown, but within a month (as quick as that) Jessie died.

She never saw the Greek boy any more. Indeed, his father had lost his license, "due to several complaints by the mothers of children, backed by the Woman's Club," that he was selling tainted ice cream. Mrs. Art Studevant had started a campaign to rid the town of objectionable tradespeople and question-able characters. Greeks were bound to be one or the other. For a while they even closed up Pa Jenkins' favorite bootlegger. Mrs. Studevant thought this would please Cora, but Cora only said, "Pa's been drinkin' so long he just as well keep on." She refused further to remark on her employer's campaign of purity. In the midst of this clean-up Jessie died.

On the day of the funeral, the house was stacked with flow-ers. (They held the funeral, not at the church, but at home, on account of old Grandma Studevant's infirmities.) All the fam-ily dressed in deep mourning. Mrs. Art was prostrate. As the hour for the services approached, she revived, however, and ate an omelette, "to help me go through the afternoon."

"And Cora," she said, "cook me a little piece of ham with it. I feel so weak."

"Yes, m'am."

The senior class from the high school came in a body. The Woman's Club came with their badges. The Reverend Doctor McElroy had on his highest collar and longest coat. The choir sat behind the coffin, with a special soloist to sing "He Feedeth His Flocks Like a Shepherd." It was a beautiful Spring afternoon, and a beautiful funeral.

Except that Cora was there. Of course, her presence created no comment (she was the family servant), but it was what she did, and how she did it, that has remained the talk of Melton to this day—for Cora was not humble in the face of death.

When the Reverend Doctor McElroy had finished his eulogy, and the senior class had read their memorials, and the songs had been sung, and they were about to allow the relatives and friends to pass around for one last look at Jessie Studevant, Cora got up from her seat by the dining-room door. She said, "Honey, I want to say something." She spoke as if she were addressing Jessie. She approached the coffin and held out her brown hands over the white girl's body. Her face moved in agitation. People sat stone-still and there was a long pause. Suddenly she screamed. "They killed you! And for nothin'....They killed your child....They took you away from here in the Springtime of your life, and now you'se gone, gone, gone!"

Folks were paralyzed in their seats.

Cora went on: "They preaches you a pretty sermon and they don't say nothin'. But Cora's here, honey, and she's gone tell 'em what they done to you. She's gonna tell 'em why they took you to Kansas City."

A loud scream rent the air. Mrs. Art fell back in her chair, stiff as a board. Cousin Nora and sister Mary sat like stones.

The men of the family rushed forward to grab Cora. They stumbled over wreaths and garlands. Before they could reach her, Cora pointed her long fingers at the women in black and said, "They killed you, honey. They killed you and your child. I told 'em you loved it, but they didn't care. They killed it before it was…"

A strong hand went around Cora's waist. Another grabbed her arm. The Studevant males half pulled, half pushed her through the aisles of folding chairs, through the crowded dining-room, out into the empty kitchen, through the screen door into the backyard. She struggled against them all the way, accusing their women. At the door she sobbed, great tears coming for the love of Jessie.

She sat down on a wash bench in the backyard, crying. In the parlor she could hear the choir singing weakly. In a few moments she gathered herself together, and went back into the house. Slowly, she picked up her few belongings from the kitchen and pantry, her aprons and her umbrella, and went off down the alley, home to Ma. Cora never came back to work for the Studevants.

Now she and Ma live from the little garden they raise, and from the junk Pa collects—when they can take by main force a part of his meager earnings before he buys his licker.

Anyhow, on the edge of Melton, the Jenkins niggers, Pa and Ma and Cora, somehow manage to get along.

From
Night Story

Babs H. Deal

"I DON'T THINK THERE'S ANY NEED OF ME GOING IN with you, is there?" Carter McCain said to the girl beside him.

"Yes you are too," Estelle Harris said. "You don't think I'd go by myself?"

She was a dark girl with wide brown eyes and a patrician nose that contrasted with her full, too-wide mouth. She wore her hair long, which emphasized her smallness. "You just say you're my husband. You'll probably have to sign something, I've heard."

"I don't want to do that," Carter said.

"You promised Dupree," Estelle said, pouting.

"Are you scared?" Carter said.

"Yeah. Sort of. I mean like going to the dentist, scared. But not as scared as I'd be not to. That's for sure. Come on now, Carter. You got to go in with me."

"O.K. Let me have a cigarette first." He reached behind the sun visor for the pack. "You want one?"

"All right." She accepted the cigarette and sat smoking, looking out the window at the white bungalow with the porch swing and the potted plants on the banisters. "It don't look like the kind of place it is," she said finally.

Carter laughed. "You expect them to advertise?" he said.

He was embarrassed and unhappy but he had accepted the commission for Dupree and he couldn't get out of it. The only thing he knew to do was see it through and get home quick. It wasn't really any concern of his anyway. He had no right or reason to make judgments. It was a favor he was doing for a friend and for a few bucks, and that was all. But he hated it anyway.

He looked at Estelle beside him, pretty, vain, irresponsible, and he tried to think of Laura Lee. But the image wouldn't come to him. Laura Lee didn't belong here. But he did. This was a place where Carter McCain would logically find himself. And it was no sort of place for Laura Lee to ever be. It scared him, thinking like that. It put something between him and Laura Lee that he didn't want to see. It put him squarely where he belonged, on the night side of the world, and left Laura Lee where she belonged, in the daylight. That was how he always thought of her anyway. The small blonde image was always surrounded by sunlight in his mind. And that was very odd because he didn't think he'd ever seen her in sunlight. He didn't live in sunlight himself. When the sun was up he slept, when the lights came on in the darkness his day began. It was like that for him and for his family and for all his friends. They belonged to the night just like ole Blackjack Ferguson did. Although the day people might collide with them in the hours between dark and midnight, there were the long stretches of daytime that belonged only to them, just as there was the dense stretch of midnight to dawn that belonged to him and his kind. The meeting place wasn't enough to change that.

He watched the smoke on his cigarette, trying to eke it out, make it last a little longer. Being of the night was more than just a matter of employment. There were certain people who had to be that way. That was why they worked at night. Dupree and Estelle and their all-night café, Arlie Machen and his filling station, Ferguson, the other taxi drivers, his parents with their whiskey. And the others, those who didn't work at night at all, but lived that way all the same: his Uncle Jake and Julie Hobson. They could have slept at night and lived in the sun, but they didn't want to. And what did Laura Lee really want? He didn't know.

"You ready?" Estelle said.

"All right." He got out of the car and stretched, feeling his body taut after the long drive. It was a good body, and it behaved well for him. He was a little too thin, maybe, but the muscle was all right. "Come on," he said. "Let's get it over with."

The door was bare and plain, an ordinary door. He knocked and a Negro woman answered it and called over her shoulder. "Miz Myerson. These folks here."

Mrs. Myerson came out of the living room. She looked like somebody's mother or grandmother, a fat placid woman with short gray hair and a pleasant face. "You the folks from Alabama?" she said.

"That's right," Carter said.

Beside him Estelle seemed to have lost some of her nonchalance. Carter put a hand on her shoulder and patted her. He felt very out of place.

"Sit down, please," Mrs. Myerson said. She walked over to the door and flipped the night latch on. "That's all, Gertrude," she said to the colored woman. Then she motioned them in front of her through an archway into the living room. She sat down in an old-fashioned rocking chair and folded her hands across her stomach. "You the husband?" she said.

"Yes," Carter said.

47

"All right. I want to talk to her by herself first," she said.

"No," Estelle said.

She looked at her. "All right. I always ask if you're sure you want to go through with this before I do it. Are you sure?"

Estelle whimpered suddenly, a small sound, lost in the creaking rockers. Then she cleared her throat. "I'm sure," she said.

"It'll be two hundred dollars—cash," the woman said.

Estelle opened her pocketbook, a tooled leather box with fringed edges. She fumbled in it for a moment and took out a billfold fat with snapshots. She took out the two hundred dollars in twenty-dollar bills and handed it to the woman. Mrs. Myerson took the money and went to a big businesslike desk flanked by steel filing cabinets. She took a blank form out of a drawer and handed it to Carter. "Both of you sign it. Right there," she said.

Carter read the small printed form. It stated that the undersigned came here of their own accord and agreed to say nothing of the matter. He signed, watching his hand make the letters Dupree Harris in mild surprise. Estelle signed it quickly without reading it.

"You go on out on the side porch there," the woman said. She patted Estelle's shoulder and pushed her toward a door that led to the back of the house. Carter went to the porch. He was glad to get there. There were potted plants here too and a glider. He sat down, wondering how long it would take.

It didn't take long. In what seemed only a few minutes Estelle was standing in the door looking at him. She was very pale, her face drawn a little. "Let's get out of here," she said.

"Are you all right?"

She nodded. "Fine. My ears sort of ring. That's all. You come on now, Carter. I don't like it here. I want to go home."

"All right."

Mrs. Myerson was standing by the front door, holding it open. She had a prescription blank in her hand and she handed it to Carter. "You can get this in the drugstore next door," she said. "It's just something to keep her from feeling sick at her stomach. That's all I can get you. If she needs something later I've already told her to try whiskey. Keep her walking. Don't let her go to bed. You hear me?"

"All right," Carter said.

"She told me that," Estelle said. "Come on. I want to get out of here." She went out the door and he followed her. She got in the car and slammed the door behind her. Carter went around and got in under the wheel. "We better go next door here and get this for you," he said.

"All right." She was sitting quiet, her eyes shut, something clutched in her hand. Carter looked down. It was her pants, white with lace on them. It made him feel terrible. He swallowed.

"Estelle," he said. "I wish Dupree was here."

She shook her head, her eyes still tightly closed. "I didn't want him here," she said. "He hates me enough for doing it. He'd never forgive me if he'd come with me."

Carter looked away from her. He backed the car out and drove the few yards to the drugstore. "You want to come in?" he said.

"Yes. Wait a minute." She bent over and eased the pants over her feet and up her legs underneath her skirt. Carter looked carefully away from her.

"I can go in and get it," he said.

"I'm coming." She opened her door and got out.

The drugstore was dim and cool. There were marble-topped tables and old-fashioned wire chairs and a tall marble counter. There was no one in the store except the druggist, a round bald man with rimless glasses. They sat down at a table and he came over. Carter handed him the prescription.

Estelle sat very still, her hands still clenched. "Estelle," Carter said. "Are you sure you're all right? We got to drive back. Maybe I ought to get you to a doctor."

"Don't be an ass," she said shortly. "I'm perfectly all right. There wasn't anything to it. It didn't hurt at all, in spite of all those things they say. I just feel sick. Sick to my stomach." She stopped and looked at Carter. "And awful. Awful. Awful. Awful. Nothing feels real and I feel dirty. There. Now shut up."

Carter looked away from her. The druggist came over with a paper cup and a small bottle. "Five bucks," he said to Carter.

Carter took the money out of his pocket and handed it to him while Estelle was still fumbling with the leather bag. The druggist grinned. Carter stared hard at him. "Bring us two cups of coffee, you s.o.b.," he said.

The druggist shrugged and walked back to the counter.

Carter leaned over and sniffed the cup. It was ordinary spirits of ammonia. "Drink it down," he said. "It won't hurt and, who knows, it might even help."

Estelle drank obediently. He looked at the bottle. Ordinary paregoric. He laughed. "They don't plan on helping you out any, do they?" he said.

"What?" Estelle focused her eyes on him. They looked bright, yet fuzzy.

"Forget it," he said. "Here's the coffee." He drank both cups because she said she couldn't drink any. Then they walked out to the car and started home.

"You want to lie down in the back seat?" Carter said.

She shook her head. "She said not to lie down and go to sleep," she said. "I feel sort of lightheaded. Turn on the radio."

"All right." He flipped the dial and the car was filled with hillbilly music. He cut down the volume. "I'll have you home in no time," he said.

"I wish you wouldn't," she said softly. "I wish we could just ride on and on and on in the night, and never get back to that damned café."

"I know a bootlegger in the next town," Carter said. "We'll stop and get you some whiskey."

"That's a good idea. I could use it."

Carter didn't answer her, concentrating on the road in front of him. He was a good driver and he was in this moment damned glad of it. He felt a little sick himself.

In the next town he stopped at a café on the outskirts and went in. He bought a pint of Seagram's and brought it back and dumped it in Estelle's lap. She broke the seal with one of her long red nails and screwed the top off. "Want one?" she said.

He shook his head. "I sure don't want to lose my license tonight," he said.

"Poor Carter," she said, laughing. "You have got a carload of trouble, haven't you? You shouldn't be so damned good to people. This is what it gets you into. You hate it, don't you? You're just like Dupree. You can't see why on earth I don't want a drooling, sloppy baby slung on one hip while I dish hash with the other hand. Poor Carter. You'd probably feel better about it if I wasn't married."

He didn't answer her, but she was right. He would feel better about it if she wasn't married. There were times when people got themselves into something they had to get out of, but this wasn't one of them. Estelle had a husband who was nuts about her. One who had taken her off a back-country farm and who spent most of his money for clothes to put on her back. He tried again to think of Laura Lee, but the image blurred. "We're making good time," he said.

Estelle tilted the bottle up again. "Maybe I wouldn't have if it had been yours," she said.

He didn't answer her.

"You hear me?" she said.

"I heard you."

"Well?"

"You're tight."

"O.K.," she said. "So I am. But it's true. Though, come to think of it, Will is probably more my type. He looks some like you, but he don't have so many… so many what?"

"Scruples?"

"That's it. Scruples. Isn't that a word?" She giggled.

"You better save some of that," Carter said. "You might need it later."

"Sure." She screwed the top on the bottle and put it in her purse.

Going up the mountain out of Fort Morgan he heard her begin to cry. He drove on up the mountain, going as fast as he dared in the darkness. When he got to the drive-in at the top of the climb he pulled in behind the building and switched off the lights. "O.K., honey," he said. "Bawl." He took a handkerchief out of his pocket, looked at it, and put it back. "You got a handkerchief?" he said.

She nodded, fumbling in her purse. He let her cry for a few minutes. Then he went in and got some coffee and ice cream.

She sat up straight when he came back to the car and smiled at him. He handed her the carton of ice cream and she ate eagerly, sniffing occasionally. Then she managed some of the coffee.

Carter stood outside the car, drinking his coffee and looking at the lights of the drive-in.

Estelle leaned over and stuck her head out the door on his side. "I'm sorry I was so bitchy, Carter," she said. "It's sort of a spooky feeling I've got. I didn't mean to take it out on you."

"Forget it. You through?" She nodded. He tossed the cartons out on the gravel and pulled back on the road. "I got to get you home before Dupree goes nuts," he said.

"All right." She leaned back against the seat and closed her eyes.

1957, a Romance

Ellen Gilchrist

IT WAS JUNE IN NORTHERN ALABAMA. UPSTAIRS RHODA'S small sons lay sleeping. Somewhere in North Carolina her young husband sulked because she'd left him.

Rhoda had the name. She had fucked her fat, balding gynecologist all Wednesday afternoon to get the name. She had fucked him on the daybed in his office and on the examining table and on the rug in the waiting room. Now all she needed was five hundred dollars.

No one was going to cut Rhoda's stomach open again. She had come home to get help. She had come home to the one person who had never let her down.

She went into the downstairs bathroom, washed her face, and went up to his room to wake him.

"I have to talk to you, Daddy," she said, touching him on the shoulder. "Come downstairs. Don't wake up mother."

They sat down together in the parlor, close together on the little sofa. He was waking up, shaking sleep from his handsome Scotch face. The old T-shirt he wore for a pajama top seemed very dear to Rhoda. She touched it while she talked.

"I have to get some money, Daddy," she said. "I'm pregnant again. I have to have an abortion. I can't stand to have another baby. I'll die if they keep cutting me open. You can't go on having cesarean sections like that."

"Oh, my," he said, his old outfielder's body going very still inside. "Does Malcolm know all this?" Usually he pretended to have forgotten her husband's name.

"No one knows. I have to do this right away, do you understand? I have to do something about it right away."

"You don't want to tell Malcolm?"

"I can't tell Malcolm. He'd never let me do it. I know that. And no one is going to stop me. He got me pregnant on purpose, Daddy. He did it because he knew I was going to leave him sooner or later."

Rhoda was really getting angry. She always believed her own stories as soon as she told them.

"We'll have to find you a doctor, Honey. It's hard to find a doctor that will do that."

"I have a doctor. I have the name of a man in Houston. A Doctor Van Zandt. A friend of mine went to him. Daddy, you have to help me with this. I'm going crazy. Imagine Malcolm doing this to me. He did it to keep me from leaving...I begged him not to."

"Oh, Honey," he said. "Please don't tell me all that now. I can't stand to hear all that. It doesn't matter. All that doesn't matter. We have to take care of you now. Let me think a minute."

He put his head down in his hands and conferred with his maker. Well, Sir, he said, I've spoiled her rotten. There's no getting around that. But she's mine and I'm sticking by her. You know I'd like to kill that little son of a bitch with my bare hands but I'll keep myself from doing it. So you help us out of this. You get us out of this one and I'll buy you a stained-glass window with nobody's name on it, or a new roof for the vestry if you'd rather.

Rhoda was afraid he'd gone back to sleep. "It's not my fault, Daddy," she said. "He made me do it. He did it to me on purpose. He did it to keep me from leaving...."

"All right, Honey," he said. "Don't think about any of that anymore. I'll take care of it. I'll call your Uncle James in the morning and check up on the doctor. We'll leave tomorrow as soon as I got things lined up."

"You're going with me," she said.

"Of course I'm going with you," he said. "We'll leave your mother with the babies. But, Rhoda, we can't tell your mother about this. I'll tell her I'm taking you to Tennessee to see the mines."

"It costs *five hundred dollars,* Daddy."

"I know that. Don't worry about that. You quit worrying about everything now and go on and try to get some sleep. I'm taking care of this. And, Rhoda..."

"Yes?"

"I really don't want your mother to know about this. She's got a lot on her mind right now. And she's not going to like this one bit."

"All right, Daddy. I don't want to tell her, anyway. Daddy, I could have a legal abortion if Malcolm would agree to it. You know that, don't you? People aren't supposed to go on having cesarean sections one right after the other. I know I could get a legal abortion. But you have to have three doctors sign the paper. And that takes too long. It might be too late by the time I do all that. And, besides, Malcolm would try to stop me. I can't take a chance on that. I think he wants to kill me."

"It's all right, Honey. I'm going to take care of it. You go to bed and get some sleep."

57

Rhoda watched him climb the stairs, sliding his hand along the polished stair rail, looking so vulnerable in his cotton pajama bottoms and his old T-shirt, with his broad shoulders and his big head and his tall, courteous body.

He had been a professional baseball player until she was born. He had been famous in the old Southern League, playing left field for the Nashville Volunteers.

There was a scrapbook full of his old clippings. Rhoda and her brothers had worn it out over the years. DUDLEY MANNING HITS ONE OVER THE FENCE. MANNING DOES IT AGAIN. DUDLEY LEADS THE LEAGUE.

You couldn't eat headlines in the 1930s, so when Rhoda was born he had given in to her mother's pleadings, quit baseball, and gone to work to make money.

He had made money. He had made 2 million dollars by getting up at four o'clock every morning and working his ass off every single day for years. And he had loved it, loved getting up before the sun rose, loved eating his quiet lonely breakfasts, loved learning to control his temper, loved being smarter and better and luckier than everyone else.

Every day he reminded himself that he was the luckiest son of a bitch in the world. And that made him humble, and other men loved him for his humility and forgave him for his success. Taped to his dresser mirror was a little saying he had cut out of a newspaper, "EVERY DAY THE WORLD TURNS UPSIDE DOWN ON SOMEONE WHO THOUGHT THEY WERE SITTING ON TOP OF IT."

He was thinking of the saying as he went back to bed. As long as nothing happens to her, he told himself. As long as she is safe.

Breakfast was terrible. Rhoda picked at her food, pretending to eat, trying to get her mother in a good mood. Her mother, whose name was Jeannie, was a gentle, religious woman who lived her life in service to her family and friends. But she had spells of fighting back against the terrible inroads they made into her small personal life. This was one of those spells.

This was the third time in two years that Rhoda had run away from her husband and come home to live. Jeannie suspected that all Rhoda really wanted was someone to take care of her babies. Jeannie spent a lot of time suspecting Rhoda of one thing or another. Rhoda was the most demanding of her four children, the only daughter, the most unpredictable, the hardest to control or understand.

"What am I supposed to tell your husband when he calls," she said, buttering toast with a shaking hand. "I feel sorry for him when he calls up. If you're leaving town I want you to call him first."

"Now, Jeannie," Rhoda's father said. "We'll only be gone a few days. Don't answer the phone if you don't want to talk to Malcolm."

"I had an appointment to get a *permanent* today," she said. "I don't know when Joseph will be able to take me again."

"Leave the children with the maids," he said. "That's what the maids are for."

"I'm not going to leave those babies alone in a house with maids for a minute," her mother said. "This is just like you, Rhoda, coming home brokenhearted one day and going off leaving your children the next. I don't care what anyone says, Dudley, she has to learn to accept some responsibility for something."

"She's going with me to the mines," he said, getting up and putting his napkin neatly into his napkin holder. "I want her to see where the money comes from."

"Well, I'll call and see if Laura'll come over while I'm gone," Jeannie said, backing down as she always did. Besides, she loved Rhoda's little boys, loved to hold their beautiful strong bodies in her arms, loved to bathe and dress and feed them, to read to them and make them laugh and watch them play. When she was alone with them she forgot they were not her very own. Flesh of my flesh, she would think, touching their perfect skin, which was the color of apricots and wild honey, flesh of my flesh, bone of my bone.

"Oh, go on then," she said. "But please be back by Saturday."

They cruised out of town in the big Packard he had bought secondhand from old Dr. Purcell and turned onto the Natchez Trace going north.

"Where are we going?" she said.

"We have to go to Nashville to catch a plane," he said. "It's too far to drive. Don't worry about it, Honey. Just leave it to me. I've got all my ducks in a row."

"Did you call the doctor?" she said. "Did you call Uncle James?"

"Don't worry about it. I told you I've got it all taken care of. You take a nap or something."

"All right," she said, and pulled a book out of her handbag. It was Ernest Hemingway's new book, and it had come from the book club the day she left North Carolina. She had been waiting for it to come for weeks. Now she opened it to the first page, holding it up to her nose and giving it a smell.

"Across the River and into the Trees," she said. "What a wonderful title. Oh, God, he's my favorite writer." She settled further down into the seat. "This is going to be a good one. I can tell."

"Honey, look out the window at where you're going," her

father said. "This is beautiful country. Don't keep your nose in a book all your life."

"This is a new book by Ernest Hemingway," she said. "I've been waiting for it for weeks."

"But look at this country," he said. "Your ancestors came this way when they settled this country. This is how they came from Tennessee."

"They did not," she said. "They came on a boat down the river from Pennsylvannia. Momma said so."

"Well, I knew you'd have something smart-alecky to say," he said.

"The first book I read by Ernest Hemingway was last year when I was nursing Bobby," she said. "It was about this man and woman in Paris that loved each other but something was wrong with him, he got hurt in the war and couldn't make love to her. Anyway, she kept leaving him and going off with other men. It was so sad I cried all night after I read it. After that I read all his books as fast as I could."

"I don't know why you want to fill up your head with all that stuff," he said. "No wonder you don't have any sense, Rhoda."

"Well, never mind that," she said. "Oh, good, this is really going to be good. It's dedicated 'To Mary, With Love,' that's his wife. She's terrible looking. She doesn't wear any makeup and she's got this terrible wrinkled skin from being in the sun all the time. I saw a picture of her in a magazine last year. I don't know what he sees in her."

"Maybe she knows how to keep her mouth shut," he said. "Maybe she knows how to stay home and be a good wife."

"Oh, well," Rhoda said, "let's don't talk about that. I don't feel like talking about that."

"I'm sorry, Honey," he said. "You go on and read your

book." He set the speedometer on an easy sixty miles an hour and tried not to think about anything. Outside the window the hills of north Alabama were changing into the rich fields of Tennessee. He remembered coming this way as a young man, driving to Nashville to play ball, dreaming of fame, dreaming of riches. He glanced beside him, at the concentrated face of his beautiful spoiled crazy daughter.

Well, she's mine, he told himself. And nothing will ever hurt her. As long as I live nothing will ever harm her.

He sighed, letting out his breath in a loud exhalation, but Rhoda could not hear him now. She was far away in the marshes near Tagliamento, in northern Italy, hunting ducks at dawn with Ernest Hemingway. (Rhoda was not fooled by personas. In her mind any modern novel was the true story of the writer's life.)

Rhoda was reading as they went into the Nashville airport and she kept on reading while they waited for the plane, and as soon as she was settled in her seat she found her place and went on reading.

The love story had finally started. *Then she came into the room, shining in her youth and tall striding beauty, and the carelessness the wind had made of her hair. She had pale, almost olive colored skin, a profile that could break your, or anyone else's heart, and her dark hair, of a thick texture, hung down over her shoulders.*

"*Hello, my great beauty,*" the Colonel said.

This was more like it, Rhoda thought. This was a better girlfriend for Ernest Hemingway than his old wife. She read on. Renata was nineteen! Imagine that! Ernest Hemingway's girlfriend was the same age as Rhoda! Imagine being in Venice with a wonderful old writer who was about to die of a heart attack. Imagine making love to a man like that. Rhoda imagined herself in a wonderful bed in a hotel in Venice making love all night to a dying author who could fuck like a nineteen-year-old boy.

She raised her eyes from the page. "Did you get Uncle James on the phone?" she said. "Did you ask him to find out about the doctor?"

"He told me what to do," her father said. "He said first you should make certain you're pregnant."

"I'm certain," she said. "I even know why. A rubber broke. It was Malcolm's birthday and I was out of jelly and I told him I didn't want to…"

"Oh, Honey, please don't talk like that. Please don't tell me all that."

"Well, it's the truth," she said. "It's the reason we're on this plane."

"Just be quiet and go on and read your book then," he said. He went back to his newspaper. In a minute he decided to try again.

"James said the doctor will have to know for certain that you're pregnant."

"All right," she said. "I'll think up something to tell him. What do you think we should say my name is?"

"Now, Sweetie, don't start that," he said. "We're going to tell this man the truth. We're not doing anything we're ashamed of."

"Well, we can't tell him I'm married," she said. "Or else he'll make me get my husband's permission."

"Where'd you get an idea like that?" he said.

"Stella Mabry told me. She tried to get an abortion last year, but she didn't take enough money with her. You have to say you're divorced."

"All right," he said. "I'll tell you what, Honey. You just let me talk to the man. You be quiet and I'll do the talking."

He lay back and closed his eyes, hoping he wasn't going to end up vomiting into one of the Southern Airlines' paper bags.

He was deathly afraid to fly and had only been on an airplane once before in his life.

A taxi took them to the new Hilton. Rhoda had never been in such a fancy hotel. She had run away to get married when she was seventeen years old and her only vacations since then had been to hospitals to have babies.

The bellboy took them upstairs to a suite of rooms. There were two bedrooms and a large living room with a bar in one corner. It looked like a movie set, with oversize beige sofas and a thick beige tweed carpet. Rhoda looked around approvingly and went over to the bar and fixed herself a tall glass of ice water.

Her father walked out onto the balcony and called to her. "Rhoda, look out here. That's an Olympic-size swimming pool. Isn't that something? The manager said some Olympic swimmers had been working out here in the afternoons. Maybe we'll get to watch them after a while."

She looked down several stories to the bright blue rectangle. "Can I go swimming in it?" she said.

"Let's call the doctor first and see what he wants us to do." He took a phone number from his billfold, sat down in a chair with his back to her, and talked for a while on the phone, nodding his head up and down as he talked.

"He said to come in first thing in the morning. He gets there at nine."

"Then I'll go swimming until dinner," she said.

"Fine," he said. "Did you bring a swimsuit?"

"Oh, no," she said. "I didn't think about it."

"Well, here," he said, handing her a hundred dollar bill. "Go find a gift shop and see if they don't have one that will fit you. And buy a robe to go over it. You can't go walking around a hotel in a swimsuit. I'll take a nap while you're gone. I'll come down and find you later."

She went down to the ground floor and found the gift shop, a beautiful little glassed-in area that smelled of cool perfume and was presided over by an elegant woman with her hair up in a bun.

Rhoda tried on five or six swimming suits and finally settled on a black one-piece maillot cut low in the back. She admired herself in the mirror. Two weeks of being too worried to eat had melted the baby fat from her hips and stomach, and she was pleased with the way her body looked.

While she admired herself in the mirror the saleslady handed her a beach robe. It was a black-and-white geometric print that came down to the floor.

"This is the latest thing in the Caribbean," the saleslady said. "It's the only one I have left. I sold one last week to a lady from New York."

"It's darling," Rhoda said, wrapping it around her, imagining what Ernest Hemingway would think if he could see her in this. "But it's too long."

"How about a pair of Wedgies," the saleslady said. "I've got some on sale."

Rhoda added a pair of white canvas Wedgies to her new outfit, collected the clothes she had been wearing in a shopping bag, paid for her purchases, and went out to sit by the pool.

The swimming team had arrived and was doing warm-up laps. A waiter came, and she ordered a Coke and sipped it while she watched the beautiful young bodies of the athletes. There was a blond boy whose shoulders reminded her of her husband's and she grew interested in him, wondering if he was a famous Olympic swimmer. He looked like he would be a lot of fun, not in a bad mood all the time like Malcolm. She kept looking at him until she caught his eye and he smiled at her. When he dove back into the pool she reached under the table and took off her wedding ring and slipped in into her pocketbook.

When she woke up early the next morning her father was already up, dressed in a seersucker suit, talking on the phone to his mine foreman in Tennessee.

"I can't believe I'm going to be through with all this today," she said, giving him a kiss on the forehead. "I love you for doing this for me, Daddy. I won't ever forget it as long as I live."

"Well, let's just don't talk about it too much," he said. "Here, look what's in the paper. Those sapsuckers in Washington are crazy as loons. We haven't been through with Korea four years and they're fixing to drag us into this mess in Vietnam. Old Douglas MacArthur told them not to get into a land war in Asia, but nobody would listen to him."

"Let me see," Rhoda said, taking the newspaper from him. She agreed with her father that the best way to handle foreign affairs was for the United States to divide up the world with Russia. "They can boss half and we'll boss half," he had been preaching for years. "Because that's the way it's going to end up anyway."

*

Rhoda's father was in the habit of being early to his appointments, so at eight o'clock they descended in the elevator, got into a taxi, and were driven through the streets of Houston to a tall office building in the center of town. They went up to the fifth floor and into a waiting room that looked like any ordinary city doctor's office. There was even a Currier and Ives print on the wall. Her father went in and talked to the doctor for a while, then he came to the door and asked her to join them. The doctor was a short, nervous man with thin light-colored hair and a strange smell about him. Rhoda thought he smelled like a test tube. He sat beside an old rolltop desk and asked her questions, half-listening to the answers.

"I'm getting a divorce right away," Rhoda babbled, "my husband forced me to make love to him and I'm not supposed to have any more babies because I've already had two cesarean sections in twelve months and I could have a legal abortion if I wanted to but I'm afraid to wait as long as it would take to get permission. I mean I'm only nineteen and what would happen to my babies if I died. Anyway, I want you to know I think you're a real humanitarian for doing this for people. I can't tell you what it meant to me to even find out your name. Do you remember Stella Mabry that came here last year? Well, anyway, I hope you're going to do this for me because I think I'll just go crazy if you don't."

"Are you sure you're pregnant?" he asked.

"Oh, yes," she said. "I'm sure. I've missed a period for three and a half weeks and I've already started throwing up. That's why I'm so sure. Look, I just had two babies in thirteen months. I know when I'm pregnant. Look at the circles under my eyes. And I've been losing weight. I always lose weight at first. Then I blow up like a balloon." Oh, God, she thought. Please let him believe me. Please make him do it.

"And another thing," she said. "I don't care what people say about you. I think you are doing a great thing. There will be a time when everyone will know what a great service you're performing. I don't care what anyone says about what you're doing…"

"Honey," her father said. "Just answer his questions."

"When was your last period," the doctor said. He handed her a calendar and she picked out a date and pointed to it.

Then he gave her two small white pills to swallow and a nurse came and got her and helped her undress and she climbed up on an operating table and everything became very still and dreamy and the nurse was holding her hand. "Be still," the nurse said. "It won't take long."

She saw the doctor between her parted legs with a mask tied around his face and an instrument in his hand and she thought for a moment he might be going to kill her, but the nurse squeezed her hand and she looked up at the ceiling and thought of nothing but the pattern of the tiles revolving around the light fixture.

They began to pack her vagina with gauze. "Relax," the nurse said. "It's all over."

"I think you are wonderful," she said in a drowsy voice. "I think you are a wonderful man. I don't care what anyone says about you. I think you are doing a great service to mankind. Someday everyone will know what a good thing you're doing for people."

When she woke up her father was with her and she walked in a dream out of the offices and into the elevator and down to the tiled foyer and out onto the beautiful streets of the city. The sun was brilliant and across the street from the office building was a little park with the sound of a million crickets rising and falling in the sycamore trees. And all the time a song was playing inside of her. "I don't have to have a baby, I don't have to have a baby, I don't have to have a baby."

"Oh, God, oh, thank you so much," she said, leaning against her father. "Oh, thank you, oh, thank you so much. Oh, thank you, thank you, thank you."

He took her to the hotel and put her into the cool bed and covered her with blankets and sat close beside her in a chair all afternoon and night while she slept. The room was dark and cool and peaceful, and whenever she woke up he was there beside her and nothing could harm her ever as long as he lived. No one could harm her or have power over her or make her do anything as long as he lived.

All night he was there beside her, in his strength and goodness, as still and gentle as a woman.

All night he was there, half-asleep in his chair. Once in the night she woke up hungry and room service brought a steak and some toast and milk and he fed it to her bite by bite. Then he gave her another one of the pills, put the glass of milk to her lips, and she drank deeply of the cold, lush liquid, then fell back into a dreamless sleep.

The plane brought them to Nashville by noon the next day, and they got into the Packard and started driving home.

He had made a bed for her in the back seat with pillows for her head and his raincoat for a cover and she rode along that way, sleeping and reading her book. The wad of gauze in her vagina was beginning to bother her. It felt like a thick hand inside her body. The doctor had said she could remove it in twenty-four hours, but she was afraid to do it yet.

Well, at least that's over, she thought. At least I don't have to have any more babies this year.

All I have to do is have one more and they'll give me a tubal ligation. Doctor Greer promised me that. On the third cesarean section you get to have your tubes cut. It's a law. They have to do it. It would be worth having another baby for that. Oh, well, she thought. At least I don't have to worry about it anymore for now. She opened her book.

"You are not that kind of soldier and I am not that kind of girl," Renata was saying to Colonel Cantrell. *"But sometime give me something lasting that I can wear and be happy each time I wear it."*

"I see," the Colonel said. *"And I will."*

"You learn fast about things you do not know," the girl said. *"And you make lovely quick decisions. I would like you to have the emeralds and you could keep them in your pocket like a lucky piece, and feel them if you were lonely."*

Rhoda fell asleep, dreaming she was leaning across a table staring into Ernest Hemingway's eyes as he lit her cigarette.

When they got to the edge of town he woke her. "How are you feeling, Honey," he said. "Do you feel all right?"

"Sure," she said. "I feel great, really I do."

"I want to go by the house on Manley Island if you feel like it," he said. "Everyone's out there."

It's the Fourth of July, she thought. I had forgotten all about it. Every year her father's large Scotch family gathered for the Fourth on a little peninsula that jutted out into the Tennessee River a few miles from town.

"Will Jamie be there?" she asked. Jamie was everyone's favorite. He was going to be a doctor like his father.

"I think so. Do you feel like going by there?"

"Of course I do," she said. "Stop and let me get into the front seat with you."

They drove up into a yard full of automobiles. The old summer house was full of cousins and aunts and uncles, all carrying drinks and plates of fried chicken and all talking at the same time.

Rhoda got out of the car feeling strange and foreign and important, as if she were a visitor from another world, arriving among her kinfolk carrying an enormous secret that they could not imagine, not even in their dreams.

She began to feel terriby elated, moving among her cousins, hugging and kissing them.

Then her Uncle James came and found her. He was an eye surgeon. Her father had paid his tuition to medical school when there was barely enough money to feed Rhoda and her brothers.

"Let's go for a walk and see if any of Cammie's goats are still loose in the woods," he said, taking hold of her arm.

"I'm fine," she said. "I'm perfectly all right, Uncle James."

"Well, just come walk with me and tell me about it," he said. They walked down the little path that led away from the house to the wild gardens and orchards at the back of the property. He had his hand on her arm. Rhoda loved his hands, which were always unbelievably clean and smelled wonderful when they came near you.

"Tell me about it," he said.

"There isn't anything to tell," she said. "They put me up on an examining table and first they gave me some pills and they made me sleepy and they said it might hurt a little but it didn't hurt and I slept a long time afterwards. Well, first we went down in an elevator and then we went back to the hotel and I slept until this morning. I can't believe that was only yesterday."

"Have you been bleeding?"

"Not a lot. Do you think I need some penicillin? He was a real doctor, Uncle James. There were diplomas on the wall and a picture of his family. What about the penicillin? Should I take it just in case?"

"No. I think you're going to be fine. I'm going to stay around for a week just in case."

"I'm glad you came. I wanted to see Jamie. He's my favorite cousin. He's getting to be so handsome. I'll bet the girls are crazy about him."

"Tell me this," he said. "Did the doctor do any tests to see if you were pregnant?"

"I know I was pregnant," she said. "I was throwing up every morning. Besides, I've been pregnant for two years. I guess I know when I'm pregnant by now."

"You didn't have tests made?"

"How could I? I would have had to tell somebody. Then they might have stopped me."

"I doubt if you were really pregnant," he said. "I told your father I think it's highly unlikely that you were really pregnant."

"I know I was pregnant."

"Rhoda, listen to me. You don't have any way of knowing that. The only way you can be sure is to have the tests and it would be doing your father a big favor if you told him you weren't sure of it. I think you imagined you were pregnant because you dread it so much."

Rhoda looked at his sweet impassive face trying to figure

out what he wanted from her, but the face kept all its secrets.

"Well, it doesn't matter to me whether I was or not," she said. "All I care about is that it's over. Are you sure I don't need any penicillin? I don't want to get blood poisoning."

(Rhoda was growing tired of the conversation. It isn't any of his business what I do, she thought, even if he is a doctor.)

She left him then and walked back to the house, glancing down every now and then at her flat stomach, running her hand across it, wondering if Jamie would like to take the boat up to Guntersville Dam to go through the locks.

Her mother had arrived from town with the maid and her babies and she went in and hugged them and played with them for a minute, then she went into the bathroom and gingerly removed the wad of bloody gauze and put in a tampon.

She washed her legs and rubbed hand lotion on them and then she put on the new black bathing suit. It fit better than ever.

"I'm beautiful," she thought, running her hands over her body. "I'm skinny and I'm beautiful and no one is ever going to cut me open. I'm skinny and I'm beautiful and no one can make me do anything."

She began to laugh. She raised her hand to her lips and great peals of clear abandoned laughter poured out between her fingers, filling the tiny room, laughing back at the wild excited face in the bright mirror.

From
The Abortion:
An Historical Romance, 1966

Richard Brautigan

MY FIRST ABORTION

ABOUT FOREVER OR TEN MINUTES PASSED AND THEN
the doctor came back and motioned toward Vida and me to
come with him, though the other people had been waiting
when we came in. Perhaps it had something to do with Foster.

"Please," Dr. Garcia said, quietly.

We followed after him across the hall and into a small
office. There was a desk in the office and a typewriter. The
office was dark and cool, the shades were down, with a leather
chair and photographs of the doctor and his family upon the
walls and the desk.

There were various certificates showing the medical
degrees the doctor had obtained and what schools he had
graduated from.

There was a door that opened directly into an operating
room. A teen-age girl was in the room cleaning up and a
young boy, another teen-ager, was helping her.

A big blue flash of fire jumped across a tray full of surgical
instruments. The boy was sterilizing the instruments with
fire. It startled Vida and me. There was a table in the operating room that had metal things to hold your legs and there
were leather straps that went with them.

75

"No pain," the doctor said to Vida and then to me. "No pain and clean, all clean, no pain. Don't worry. No pain and clean. Nothing left. I'm a doctor," he said.

I didn't know what to say. I was so nervous that I was almost in shock. All the color had drained from Vida's face and her eyes looked as if they could not see any more.

"250 dollars," the doctor said. "Please."

"Foster said it would be 200 dollars. That's all we have," I heard my own voice saying. "200. That's what you told Foster."

"200. That's all you have?" the doctor said.

Vida stood there listening to us arbitrate the price of her stomach. Vida's face was like a pale summer cloud.

"Yes," I said. "That's all we have."

I took the money out of my pocket and gave it to the doctor. I held the money out and he took it from my hand. He put it in his pocket, without counting it, and then he became a doctor again, and that's the way he stayed all the rest of the time we were there.

He had only stopped being a doctor for a moment. It was a little strange. I don't know what I expected. It was very good that he stayed a doctor for the rest of the time.

Foster was of course right.

He became a doctor by turning to Vida and smiling and saying, "I won't hurt you and it will be clean. Nothing left after and no pain, honey. Believe me. I'm a doctor."

Vida smiled ½: ly.

"How long has she been?" the doctor said to me and starting to point at her stomach but not following through with it, so his hand was a gesture that didn't do anything.

"About five or six weeks," I said.

Vida was now smiling ¼: ly.

The doctor paused and looked at a calendar in his mind and

then he nodded affectionately at the calendar. It was probably a very familiar calendar to him. They were old friends.

"No breakfast?" he said, starting to point again at Vida's stomach but again he failed to do so.

"No breakfast," I said.

"Good girl," the doctor said.

Vida was now smiling $1/37$: ly.

After the boy finished sterilizing the surgical instruments, he took a small bucket back through another large room that was fastened to the operating room.

The other room looked as if it had beds in it. I moved my head a different way and I could see a bed in it and there was a girl lying on the bed asleep and there was a man sitting in a chair beside the bed. It looked very quiet in the room.

A moment after the boy left the operating room, I heard a toilet flush and water running from a tap and then the sound of water being poured in the toilet and the toilet was flushed again and the boy came back with the bucket.

The bucket was empty.

The boy had a large gold wristwatch on his hand.

"Everything's all right," the doctor said.

The teen-age girl, who was dark and pretty and also had a nice wristwatch, came into the doctor's office and smiled at Vida. It was that kind of smile that said: It's time now; please come with me.

"No pain, no pain, no pain," the doctor repeated like a nervous nursery rhyme.

No pain, I thought, how strange.

"Do you want to watch?" the doctor asked me, gesturing toward an examination bed in the operating room where I could sit if I wanted to watch the abortion.

I looked over at Vida. She didn't want me to watch and I didn't want to watch either.

"No," I said. "I'll stay in here."

"Please come, honey," the doctor said.

The girl touched Vida's arm and Vida went into the operating room with her and the doctor closed the door, but it didn't really close. It was still open an inch or so.

"This won't hurt," the girl said to Vida. She was giving Vida a shot.

Then the doctor said something in Spanish to the boy who said OK and did something.

"Take off your clothes," the girl said. "And put this on."

Then the doctor said something in Spanish and the boy answered him in Spanish and the girl said, "Please. Now put your legs up. That's it. Good. Thank you."

"That's right, honey," the doctor said. "That didn't hurt, did it? Everything's going to be all right. You're a good girl."

Then he said something to the boy in Spanish and then the girl said something in Spanish to the doctor who said something in Spanish to both of them.

Everything was very quiet for a moment or so in the operating room. I felt the dark cool of the doctor's office on my body like the hand of some other kind of doctor.

"Honey?" the doctor said. "Honey?"

There was no reply.

Then the doctor said something in Spanish to the boy and the boy answered him in something metallic, surgical. The doctor used the thing that was metallic and surgical and gave it back to the boy who gave him something else that was metallic and surgical.

Everything was either quiet or metallic and surgical in there for a while.

Then the girl said something in Spanish to the boy who replied to her in English, "I know," he said.

The doctor said something in Spanish.

The girl answered him in Spanish.

A few moments passed during which there were no more surgical sounds in the room. There was now the sound of cleaning up and the doctor and the girl and the boy talked in Spanish as they finished up.

Their Spanish was not surgical any more. It was just casual cleaning-up Spanish.

"What time is it?" the girl said. She didn't want to look at her watch.

"Around one," the boy said.

The doctor joined them in English. "How many more?" he said.

"Two," the girl said.

"¿Dos?" the doctor said in Spanish.

"There's one coming," the girl said.

The doctor said something in Spanish.

The girl answered him in Spanish.

"I wish it was three," the boy said in English.

"Stop thinking about girls," the doctor said, jokingly.

Then the doctor and the girl were involved in a brief very rapid conversation in Spanish.

This was followed by a noisy silence and then the sound of the doctor carrying something heavy and unconscious out of the operating room. He put the thing down in the other room and came back a moment later.

The girl walked over to the door of the room I was in and finished opening it. My dark cool office was suddenly flooded with operating room light. The boy was cleaning up.

"Hello," the girl said, smiling. "Please come with me."

She casually beckoned me through the operating room as if it were a garden of roses. The doctor was sterilizing his surgical instruments with the blue flame.

He looked up at me from the burning instruments and said, "Everything went OK. I promised no pain, all clean. The usual." He smiled. "Perfect."

The girl took me into the other room where Vida was lying unconscious on the bed. She had warm covers over her. She looked as if she were dreaming in another century.

"It was an excellent operation," the girl said. "There were no complications and it went as smoothly as possible. She'll wake up in a little while. She's beautiful, isn't she?"

"Yes."

The girl got me a chair and put it down beside Vida. I sat down in the chair and looked at Vida. She was so alone there in the bed. I reached over and touched her cheek. It felt as if it had just come unconscious from an operating room.

The room had a small gas heater that was burning quietly away in its own time. The room had two beds in it and the other bed where the girl had lain a short while before was now empty and there was an empty chair beside the bed, as this bed would be empty soon and the chair I was now sitting in: to be empty.

The door to the operating room was open, but I couldn't see the operating table from where I was sitting.

MY SECOND ABORTION

The door to the operating room was open, but I couldn't see the operating table from where I was sitting. A moment later they brought in the teen-age girl from the waiting room.

"Everything's going to be all right, honey," the doctor said. "This won't hurt." He gave her the shot himself.

"Please take off your clothes," the girl said.

There was a stunned silence for a few seconds that bled into the awkward embarrassed sound of the teen-age girl taking her clothes off.

After she took off her clothes, the girl assistant who was no older than the girl herself said, "Put this on."

The girl put it on.

I looked down at the sleeping form of Vida. She was wearing one, too.

Vida's clothes were folded over a chair and her shoes were on the floor beside the chair. They looked very sad because she had no power over them any more. She lay unconscious before them.

"Now put your legs up, honey," the doctor was saying. "A little higher, please. That's a good girl."

Then he said something in Spanish to the Mexican girl and she answered him in Spanish.

"I've had six months of Spanish I in high school," the teenage girl said with her legs apart and strapped to the metal stirrups of this horse of no children.

The doctor said something in Spanish to the Mexican girl and she replied in Spanish to him.

"Oh," he said, a little absentmindedly to nobody in particular. I guess he had performed a lot of abortions that day and then he said to the teen-age girl, "That's nice. Learn some more."

The boy said something very rapidly in Spanish.

The Mexican girl said something very rapidly in Spanish.

The doctor said something very rapidly in Spanish and then he said to the teen-age girl, "How do you feel, honey?"

"Nothing," she said, smiling. "I don't feel anything. Should I feel something right now?"

The doctor said something very rapidly to the boy in Spanish. The boy did not reply.

"I want you to relax," the doctor said to the teen-age girl. "Please take it easy."

All three of them had a very rapid go at it in Spanish. There seemed to be some trouble and then the doctor said something very rapidly in Spanish to the Mexican girl. He finished it by saying, "¿Como se dice treinta?"

"Thirty," the Mexican girl said.

"Honey," the doctor said. He was leaning over the teen-age girl. "I want you to count to, to thirty for us, please, honey."

"All right," she said, smiling, but for the first time her voice sounded a little tired.

It was starting to work.

"1, 2, 3, 4, 5, 6..." There was a pause here. "7, 8, 9..." There was another pause here, but it was a little longer than the first pause.

"Count to, to thirty, honey," the doctor said.

"10, 11, 12."

There was a total stop.

"Count to thirty, honey," the boy said. His voice sounded soft and gentle just like the doctor's. Their voices were the sides of the same coin.

"What comes after 12?" the teen-age girl giggled. "I know! 13." She was very happy that 13 came after 12. "14, 15, 15, 15."

"You said 15," the doctor said.

"15," the teen-age girl said.

"What's next, honey?" the boy said.

"15," the teen-age girl said very slowly and triumphantly.

"What's next, honey?" the doctor said.

"15," the girl said. "15."

"Come on, honey," the doctor said.

"What's next?" the boy said.

"What's next?" the doctor said.

The girl didn't say anything.

They didn't say anything either. It was very quiet in the room. I looked down at Vida. She was very quiet, too.

Suddenly the silence in the operating room was broken by the Mexican girl saying, "16."

"What?" the doctor said.

"Nothing," the Mexican girl said, and then the language and silences of the abortion began.

MY THIRD ABORTION

The doctor came through the room carrying the teen-age girl in his arms. Though the doctor was a small man, he was very strong and carried the girl without difficulty.

She looked very silent and unconscious. Her hair hung strangely over his arm in a blond confusion. He took the girl through the small gym and into the adjoining room where he lay her upon the dark animal-like bed.

Then he came over and closed the door to our room and went into the forward reaches of the labyrinth and came back with the girl's parents.

83

"It went perfect," he said. "No pain, all clean."

They didn't say anything to him and he came back to our room. As he passed through the door, the people were watching him and they saw Vida lying there and me sitting beside her.

I looked at them and they looked at me before the door was closed. Their faces were a stark and frozen landscape.

The boy came into the room carrying the bucket and he went into the toilet and flushed the fetus and the abortion leftovers down the toilet.

Just after the toilet flushed, I heard the flash of the instruments being sterilized by fire.

It was the ancient ritual of fire and water all over again to be all over again and again in Mexico today.

Vida still lay there unconscious. The Mexican girl came in and looked at Vida. "She's sleeping," the girl said. "It went fine."

She went back into the operating room and then the next woman came into the operating room. She was the "one" coming the Mexican girl had mentioned earlier. I didn't know what she looked like because she had come since we'd been there.

"Has she eaten today?" the doctor said.

"No," a man said sternly, as if he were talking about dropping a hydrogen bomb on somebody he didn't like.

The man was her husband. He had come into the operating room. He had decided that he wanted to watch the abortion. They were awfully tense people and the woman said only three words all the time she was there. After she had her shot, he helped her off with her clothes.

He sat down while her legs were strapped apart on the operating table. She was unconscious just about the time they finished putting her in position for the abortion because they started almost immediately.

84

This abortion was done automatically like a machine. There was very little conversation between the doctor and his helpers.

I could feel the presence of the man in the operating room. He was like some kind of statue sitting there looking on, waiting for a museum to snatch him and his wife up. I never saw the woman.

After the abortion the doctor was tired and Vida was still lying there unconscious. The doctor came into the room. He looked down at Vida.

"Not yet," he said, answering his own question.

I said no because I didn't have anything else to do with my mouth.

"It's OK," he said. "Sometimes it's like this."

The doctor looked like an awfully tired man. God only knows how many abortions he had performed that day.

He came over and sat down on the bed. He took Vida's hand and he felt her pulse. He reached down and opened one of her eyes. Her eye looked back at him from a thousand miles away.

"It's all right," he said. "She'll be back in a few moments."

He went into the toilet and washed his hands. After he finished washing his hands, the boy came in with the bucket and took care of that.

The girl was cleaning up in the operating room. The doctor had put the woman on the examination bed in the operating room.

He had quite a thing going just taking care of the bodies.

"OHHHHHHHHHH!" I heard a voice come from behind the gym door where the doctor had taken the teen-age girl. "OHHHHHHHHHH!" It was a sentimental drunken voice. It was the girl. "OHHHHHHHHHH!

"16!" she said. "I-OHHHHHHHHHH!"

Her parents were talking to her in serious, hushed tones. They were awfully respectable.

"OHHHHHHHHHHHHHHHHHHHHHH!"

They were acting as if she had gotten drunk at a family reunion and they were trying to cover up her drunkenness.

"OHHHHHHHHHHH! I feel funny!"

There was total silence from the couple in the operating room. The only sound was the Mexican girl. The boy had come back through our room and had gone somewhere else in the building. He never came back.

After the girl finished cleaning up the operating room, she went into the kitchen and started cooking a big steak for the doctor.

She got a bottle of Miller's beer out of the refrigerator and poured the doctor a big glass of it. He sat down in the kitchen. I could barely see him drinking the beer.

Then Vida started stirring in her sleep. She opened her eyes. They didn't see anything for a moment or so and then they saw me.

"Hi," she said in a distant voice.

"Hi," I said, smiling.

"I feel dizzy," she said, coming in closer.

"Don't worry about it," I said. "Everything is fine."

"Oh, that's good," she said. There.

"Just lie quietly and take it easy," I said.

The doctor got up from the table in the kitchen and came in. He was holding the glass of beer in his hand.

"She's coming back," he said.

"Yes," I said.

"Good," he said. "Good."

He took his glass of beer and went back into the kitchen and sat down again. He was very tired.

Then I heard the people in the outside gym room dressing their daughter. They were in a hurry to leave. They sounded as if they were dressing a drunk.

"I can't get my hands up," the girl said.

Her parents said something stern to her and she got her hands up in the air, but they had so much trouble putting her little brassiere on that they finally abandoned trying and the mother put the brassiere in her purse.

"OHHHHHHHHHH! I'm so dizzy," the girl said as her parents half-carried her, half-dragged her out of the place.

I heard a couple of doors close and then everything was silent, except for the doctor's lunch cooking in the kitchen. The steak was being fried in a very hot pan and it made a lot of noise.

"What's that?" Vida said. I didn't know if she was talking about the noise of the girl leaving or the sound of the steak cooking.

"It's the doctor having lunch," I said.

"Is it that late?" she said.

"Yes," I said.

"I've been out a long time," she said.

"Yes," I said. "We're going to have to leave soon but we won't leave until you feel like it."

"I'll see what I can do," Vida said.

The doctor came back into the room. He was nervous because he was hungry and tired and wanted to close the place up for a while, so he could take it easy, rest some.

Vida looked up at him and he smiled and said, "See, no pain, honey. Everything wonderful. Good girl."

Vida smiled very weakly and the doctor returned to the kitchen and his steak that was ready now.

While the doctor had his lunch, Vida slowly sat up and I helped her get dressed. She tried standing up but it was too hard, so I had her sit back down for a few moments.

While she sat there, she combed her hair and then she tried standing up again but she still didn't have it and sat back down on the bed again.

"I'm still a little rocky," Vida said.

"That's all right."

The woman in the other room had come to and her husband was dressing her almost instantly, saying, "Here. Here. Here. Here," in a painful Okie accent.

"I'm tired," the woman said, using up ⅔ of her vocabulary.

"Here," the man said, helping her put something else on.

After he got her dressed he came into our room and stood there looking for the doctor. He was very embarrassed when he saw Vida sitting on the bed, combing her hair.

"Doctor?" he said.

The doctor got up from his steak and stood in the doorway of the kitchen. The man started to walk toward the doctor, but then stopped after taking only a few steps.

The doctor came into our room.

"Yes," he said.

"I can't remember where I parked my car," the man said. "Can you call me a taxi?"

"You lost your auto?" the doctor said.

"I parked it next to Woolworth's, but I can't remember where Woolworth's is," the man said. "I can find Woolworth's if I can get downtown. I don't know where to go."

"The boy's coming back," the doctor said. "He'll take you there in his auto."

"Thank you," the man said, returning to his wife in the other room. "Did you hear that?" he said to her.

"Yes," she said, using it all up.

"We'll wait," he said.

Vida looked over at me and I smiled at her and took her hand to my mouth and kissed it.

"Let's try again," she said.

"All right," I said.

She tried it again and this time it was all right. She stood there for a few minutes and then said, "I've got it. Let's go."

"Are you sure you have it?" I said.

"Yes."

I helped Vida on with her sweater. The doctor looked at us from the kitchen. He smiled but he didn't say anything. He had done what he was supposed to do and now we did what we were supposed to do. We left.

We wandered out of the room into the gym and worked our way to the front of the place, passing through layers of coolness to the door.

Even though it had remained a gray overcast day, we were stunned by the light and everything was instantly noisy, carlike, confused, poor, rundown and Mexican.

It was as if we had been in a time capsule and now were released again to be in the world.

The children were still playing in front of the doctor's office and again they stopped their games of life to watch two squint-eyed gringos holding, clinging, holding to each other walk up the street and into a world without them.

Acts of Violence

Zöe Fairbairns

ALTHOUGH IT WAS DOROTHY WHO HAD COME TO INTER-
view the officials at PopCon ("an Intergovernmental Agency
for Fundamental Research into the Worldwide Problems of
Population Stabilization"), she kept getting the impression
that it was they who were interrogating her.

"What are you after?"

"Who do you work for—really?"

"Whose side are you on?"

"Aren't you grateful for the money?"

Dorothy explained that they hadn't given *her* any money;
she was here as a reporter for a journal whose name they
knew; her membership of the feminist abortion campaign to
which PopCon had just made a large grant was irrelevant to
the present discussion; she was just doing her job.

"Yeh, doing your job, seeing weird and wonderful conspir-
acies everywhere," said the clipped-haired, clipped-voiced
man behind the desk, the Press Liaison Officer. "Your group
better watch out. If they don't want the money—"

Dorothy scoffed. "You know quite well you can't take it
back. I just wonder why you gave it in the first place."

"And you're suggesting—"

"No, I'm *asking*. Now, are you prepared to let me look at your research program or not?"

"Not if you're going to use it for lies, propaganda, and distortion," said the Press Liaison Officer.

She got up, grinning. "I'll be off, then."

"We don't want to be obstructive, Miss Lenham, we want to help the press all we can, and there's nothing secret in what we do here, nothing whatever. But if we give you information, how do we know you won't distort it?"

"You don't," she said, sitting down. "But if you won't let me see unsecret information, I can distort *that* too."

The Press Liaison Officer took a heavy file from a shelf and almost dropped it into her hands; but she had strong wrists and managed a gracious smile of acceptance and thanks.

"My colleagues and I will be very interested," he said sourly, "to know what kind of propaganda that red magazine you work for can make out of an international survey of prospective parents' attitudes to the impending birth."

"You've got to be kidding!" yelped Margaret Lenham, as much astonished as afraid at the sight of what he planned to use for the operation: a knitting needle. A knitting needle, in this day and age! It had been good enough in the bad old days, good enough for her mother before her, good enough, in all probability, for her grandmother too, if the secrets of that angelic white head were ever known. But you expected something better nowadays, especially for a woman in her forties! "It is...clean, isn't it?"

"There's nothing to worry about, Mrs. L," he said, "I know my work." And the years rolled away, and it was a different room yet still the same, the room where she'd had her first; old white paint with the grudging cleanliness of not quite enough scrubbing; the sticky rubber mat under her bottom, that made her wonder about all the other bottoms that had lain on it, wonder desperately to take her mind off the panic at the instrument's entry into her, and the thought, *it's like the first screw you ever had—why do we do it, why do we go on doing it?*

"No," she said. "No." She felt the cold steel hesitate.

"I haven't hurt you?"

"I don't want to."

"Of course you do."

"No. I'm—we—we women, we're impulsive in middle age, you know. Change our minds a lot."

"You'll have to let me finish now that I've started," he said.

She raised her head and looked at him between her bare knees. He looked quizzical, concerned—almost personal about her. *Who the hell did he think he was?*

"Get-out-of-me!" Her body heaved, and his hurtled across the room under the unexpected blow from her foot. She fled home on the underground, scolding herself for being such a coward, it could be all over now if she'd been sensible. Or if she'd known where to go to get it done properly. She could have asked Dorothy of course, Dorothy knew about these things, but she couldn't face the look of exasperation she knew she'd get, the telling-off. She ran bleak eyes along the row of advertisements: bad breath, jobs for temps, are you pregnant? "Yes!" she said in surprise. "How clever of you—it doesn't show yet, surely?" People sitting next to her got up and moved away. She read the advertisement carefully; they helped you if you were pregnant! Well, she was going to need a lot of help, that was for sure, and if someone took the trouble to put an advert in the tube, the least you could do was memorize the

number. The things she was going to need for the baby! She
started to make a list in her head.

Dorothy, Margaret's daughter, looked round the two-room
flat that was their home, and groaned. So it had been a collection day today. Mother had been making collections. Eighteen
milk bottles on the mantelpiece, some with milky smears and
doubtless smelling cheesy. Rusty tins under the bed and a few
more in the sink. And in a carrier bag, cunningly at the back of
the cupboard, a bumper harvest of old newspapers.

Mother must have something on her mind.

"Oh *mother*— " She heard tears in her voice. She was tired.

"It's all right, dear, I'm going to wash everything, and either
keep it or sell it."

"Keep old baked bean tins?" Dorothy fought the anger that
was so debilitating, so futile. "Sell dirty newspapers?" Mother
couldn't help it. Things could be worse.

"The other way round, dear. Tins can be recycled. Perhaps
the newspapers weren't such a good idea. Not very hygienic
for—"

"OK, mother, but please clear it, and will you get dinner
tonight, I have to write something very urgently—"

Closing her mind to her mother was a survival skill Dorothy
had learned many years ago when she realized that if she didn't
look after her, no one else was going to. Then it became the only
way to work: shut mother out, shut out her demands, her out-
rages, concentrate, work. It might seem brutal sometimes, but
there was no point in having two people mad.

"...don't you think, dear?"

"Mother, I'm not discussing anything now. I'm working."
She got out her PopCon notes, started arranging things in her

mind. Start with a punchy sentence, get them reading. Then the facts, the evidence. Then the guesses, the speculations, the comments, the careful qualifications, the neat manipulation of emphasis. But which was which? Was it true? Was any of it true? Did her excitement at the way the evidence fitted together mean she wanted it to be true? And if it was true, was any purpose served by revealing it—any purpose other than the advancement of her own career?

"Dorothy, how would you feel about it if I—"

"Mother, I can't support us if I can't work."

Margaret fell silent. Dorothy was relieved. Something had apparently been decided, for Margaret's continuous muttering stopped and she went silently about the business of washing the tins. At least she only robbed bins and doorsteps, she didn't shoplift. If she screwed around, at least she was discreet. She was continent and clean and was usually OK to go out by herself. And she wasn't violent. She wasn't really violent like other mad people.

A few days later, one of the cheaper newspapers headed a story: "SCIENCE CONFIRMS: TOO MANY WOMEN!" The text said:

Science has finally confirmed what many a mere male has long suspected—that the troubles of the world are women's fault, and if there were fewer of them, things would get on a whole lot better.

This news was given to the world last night, at, of all things—a women's lib meeting!

Posing as a libber, one of our reporters attended a secret meeting of a pro-abortion group and heard its leader, journalist Miss Dorothy Lenham, warn the "sisters" that the funding given to the campaign by the prestigious international research foundation Pop-Con, might well have sinister implications.

"PopCon has been doing research all over the world to establish that the majority of prospective parents would prefer a son to a daughter, and many would be prepared to undergo minor medical procedures to ensure that they got their wish, including the abortion of a female fetus," Dorothy told a hushed audience in a room at a secret address in North London. "PopCon regards this as the final solution to the population problem, since a predominantly male population will obviously produce fewer babies than one in which the sexes are evenly matched.

"They are investing in the development of a pill that will ensure male-only births. But in the meantime, some of their researchers think it sufficient to promote sex-tests for unborn babies together with abortion on demand."

Challenged after the meeting by our reporter and asked if she was not being a bit melodramatic, Dorothy said: "It is disgraceful that you have gatecrashed a private meeting like this, and reported on thoughts that have not been fully developed yet. Wait until I've written a full report."

But did Dorothy not agree that cutting down on women might be a solution to the population problem in the third world? "Birth control isn't just about the population problem; it's about women's autonomy," she said. "We aren't breeding machines, to be phased out when no more breeding is required."

Cartoon, page 7.

Dorothy woke, tense and listening. There was someone in the corridor.

She held her breath. The lighted dial of her watch said one-twenty. Mother was drawing great rambling breaths and muttering. There was no stir in the flat. The footsteps passed on— someone for the people upstairs. Her conscience had woken her, not the footsteps. She'd hardly spoken to mother all day. She'd tried to keep the newspaper story hidden from her because she didn't want to discuss it until she'd had more time to get her thoughts in order... but of course mother had found it and started questioning compulsively about abortion, what exactly was the law on it now, how did you get one, where did you go, what did it cost, things she must have heard Dorothy and her friends discussing a hundred times but which the newspaper report had triggered into today's obsession.

Damn, damn, damn that bloody newspaper, why couldn't they give people five minutes to discuss something important without destroying everything with their hysteria and filthy ridicule?

How was a person supposed to think straight when—?

A world without women! No—not quite without. Some would be needed, there would have to be some breeding. Others would be borne by the few feminists and freaks who preferred girls, for the whole thing would be voluntary; no compulsion would be needed; PopCon's research had been thorough. In a few generations, of course, people would want girls again, and values and fashions would change…but in the meantime, what would it be like to be one of an endangered species?

What would the world be like? A universal rotary club, or army barracks, or Dartmoor prison, or Ku Klux Klan, or Catholic priesthood or boardroom or Eton or Glasgow gang! There was no lack of models.

The doorbell rang. Dorothy fled to it. Through the letter box she hissed: "Sssh, shh, please, my mother's very—"

"Dorothy. We have to talk to you."

"Who is it?"

"You don't know us."

She opened the front door and stepped out into the corridor, which was more private than the flat if mother was only pretending to be asleep, which was possible.

She faced two women, one short and tough-looking in a

military jacket; the other pale, blonde, anaemic, with watery eyes.

"We read about you in the papers," said the anaemic one.

"Who are you, though?"

"I'm Lula, this is Claire."

"I can't ask you in. My mother—"

"We have to talk somewhere," said Claire, the tough one, who was rather frightening.

"We could go for a walk," said Dorothy.

She dressed while they waited, then they went down the greasy stairs into the street. The two strangers flanked Dorothy, making her wonder, as she had at the PopCon building, whether she could get away. Not that she wanted to; the cold silence of the night was itself a release from the warm clammy room and her mother's muttered claims on her, claims from which there would be no escape until death. Three pairs of footsteps clattered on the pavement, out of step, like three clocks. Lula and Claire were talking to her, a sort of duet: Lula was persuasive and chatty, Claire chimed in with sharp ideological comments or scornful snorts: hard cop, soft cop.

"I don't know," said Dorothy softly when they wanted an answer from her. "I don't know at all."

"How can you *not know?*"

"We understand the difficulty," said Lula gently. "But we—Claire, and I, and a lot of other women—have been wondering how much longer you were going to make money writing articles about the women's movement before you felt a duty to take some kind of action."

"I didn't write that article—"

"No, they got in first, but you were planning to. You must make quite a lot of money—"

"I make my living and I support my mother!" Dorothy looked wildly around her as if for an escape—but nothing was restraining her. "I might get my arms blown off, I need them for my work! Who are you, anyway?"

"We're a group of women who are tired of talk."

"What would it achieve—supposing I did it? Why me?"

"Why you, because you know the building and could get into it. A follow-up story or something. As to what it would achieve…" Claire abandoned the explanation, Lula took her cue.

"It's symbolic. Every woman who read about what that place is for will understand. It's an act of solidarity with every woman who's under pressure to have a baby, or have a boy or have a girl or who knows, for god's sake, have a puppy or a kitten or a goddamned foal."

"I know." Dorothy bit her nails miserably. "I know. But what are we saying? All those bastards want is to let people choose the sex of their baby. What can we say against that?"

"You talk as if it was an interesting academic problem," Claire snarled. "Don't you realize they want to *wipe us out?* Can we really do nothing about it, just because they seem to have taken one of our slogans, one of our demands and twisted it? Why did you go after the story in the first place if your position wasn't clear?"

Dorothy said, "I have to live."

"So do we all, sister."

"What would I have to do…if I agreed."

"Just go in there and leave a package."

"Is that all?"

"That's all."

"OK."

*

Margaret heard Dorothy go out. Something connected with her work presumably...poor Dorothy, working all hours! Dorothy thought her efforts weren't appreciated, but oh, they were, they were. Margaret knew she wasn't the easiest person to live with, she knew she had her mad days, but Dorothy tolerated, accepted, got on with her career.

Margaret couldn't inflict a baby on her.

"Doctor, I'm pregnant."

The doctor grinned. "At your age?" He looked young enough to be her son. "You should give it up, you know," he said. "It's bad for the heart." He scribbled on a pad. "Still, a short life but a merry one, eh? Take that along to the hospital."

She got up and went to the door. She'd been in the surgery exactly two minutes. He looked up. "It was an abortion you wanted, wasn't it?"

"Yes, doctor. Thank you very much, doctor."

When she got to the hospital, they gave her an appointment to see a gynaecologist in six weeks time.

So she went instead to the place that advertised on the tube that it helped you if you were pregnant; she thought there might be the small chance that they would know where she could get an abortion. Desperation was beginning to seize at her guts; Dorothy had tolerated so much from her, but she would not take this. *Mother, I can't support us if I can't work,* she always used to say when she wanted a bit of peace and quiet...what chance of peace and quiet with a baby in the tiny flat? Dorothy would leave and abandon her at the very idea. She wasn't going to tell that fear to anyone though; she wasn't having them prying or saying that Dorothy ought to be glad of a new brother or sister.

She rang the number she'd seen on the underground and went to the address they told her.

"If you promise not to tell anyone," Margaret said, when she finally got to see a doctor. "I nearly had it done the old way, you know, with a knitting needle, then I lost my nerve."

She thought telling him that would prove she was determined.

"Would you like to tell me why you want an abortion?"

"I just do, that's all."

"Yes, but why?"

"Why do I have to tell *you?*"

"I'm the one who you're asking to do it," said the doctor, reasonably. He leaned forward. "Look, it's up to you. As far as *I'm* concerned, it's on demand. But I have to have something to go on your notes, see? Just in case we're ever investigated."

So Margaret started to tell him. Afterwards she couldn't remember half of what she'd said. If she'd meant to lie, she'd have planned the lies; as it was, it was more like someone else speaking, someone for whom all the tales might be true: the tales of the amorous husband who would not be denied, or even delayed; of her horrified discovery that her tried and trusted dutch cap had let her down after all these years, of her disappointment that she would not now be able to train as a doctor or run a campaign for more zebra crossings or offer a home to her poor ailing mother; and then of course there were the medical difficulties, what with her diabetes and the early mongol child that died and all those Caesarians; and the home where there wasn't an inch of space and how the baby would mean eviction and bankruptcy; and the fear that the baby might be too obviously of mixed-race; and the overriding, gut-rending terror that the baby might have royal blood (of course if ever this got outside these walls there would be no answering for the political consequences for the Western world); and in the circumstances it seemed kind that the child should never be born.

"Come in the day after tomorrow," he said. "You'll only have to stay one night."

He couldn't have believed all that, surely?

If she was going to be in the hospital for one night she would need lots of things to read. Or maybe they supplied them. They hadn't told her that and she would need to know. If she had to take her own reading things she ought to start collecting them now, whereas if they supplied them it would be embarrassing to turn up with a bag of newspapers, as if you didn't know how to behave. She would have to phone them. It was a stupid thing to phone to ask but she would have to. She realized in a panic that she had forgotten the number. Well— kill two birds with one stone. Down into the Central Line, pick up abandoned newspapers and look for that advertisement. She found it quite easily. It was a funny advertisement, it didn't come right out and say it gave you abortions, it just promised to "help." Why not come out and say it in this day and age, she muttered to herself as she dialed the number.

"Hello, this is Mrs. Lenham; look, about my abortion the day after tomorrow, I just wanted to know if…"

"You're having an abortion?"

"Sorry, I mean I'm pregnant and, er, you said you could help me the day after tomorrow and I wanted to know if…"

"We can help you *today*, Mrs. Lenham."

"What—?"

"The positive way."

The woman's voice made her realize something was wrong.
"You're not the place I—"

"You may have got the wrong number, dear, but it's a stroke
of luck for you…and for your baby."

"It's not a baby, it's a lump of jelly!"

Margaret panicked, she'd got the wrong number, the wrong
place, the wrong advertisement, why didn't they get off the
line, why didn't they leave her—

"It's a baby. It has arms and legs. If you were to touch him
with a pin—and he's a boy or a girl by now—he'd move away,
he feels pain. If you cut him up and pulled him out of your
body—which is what they do—"

"Oh you liar, you liar, you're lying you liar!" She banged
down the phone, rushed from the station. How dare anyone
tell her what to do? She'd choose, she'd decide, it was her
body, her life.

The fire at the PopCon building was big news for a day or so.
One office was burned out completely, and with it some fairly
important papers that would take several months' research to
restore. Seven fire engines were called, and traffic was held up
all over London. The firm which had fire-proofed the building got high praise for the containment of the blaze. It was
clearly a case of arson, but the motive was puzzling at first.
The culprit was assumed to be the young woman whose
charred body had been trapped by the flames; she was identi-
fied as a feminist—funny, when PopCon had been giving
money and moral support to feminist groups.

Then the paper that had published the earlier report recog-
nized her name as that of the rather hysterical women's libber
who was planning to expose PopCon as the enemy of women…

and this seemed to clear the matter up. Obviously a one-man operation by a disturbed girl who believed in her own propaganda.

"The cause of female freedom," warned the paper, "which we have always supported, is ill-served by terrorism of this kind."

Margaret called the new baby Dorothy Two.

With Dorothy One so suddenly dead, the abortion had been impossible.

Dorothy Two was a difficult baby. Margaret had to be anaesthetized for the birth, and she was hardly well when they sent the two of them home. Dorothy Two cried all day and cried all night, and Margaret's only respite was when she went to work, to the factory-cleaning job she had had to take. She wished Dorothy One was still there to help, but she was determined to manage. If she didn't manage they'd take the baby away, and then everything would be wasted.

She used to slip home from the factory during her lunch breaks to make sure Dorothy Two was all right. And there she'd be, always crying.

And one day a lady came from the clinic. She was a fat, plain woman in blue overalls, with moles on her face and no wedding ring.

"Good afternoon, Mrs. Lenham. We're a bit concerned about Dorothy, we haven't seen you and her for such a long time."

"She's all right."

"May I—"

"She's *asleep!*"

Dorothy Two wailed treacherously.

The clinic woman hoisted her into the air and looked at her in distaste. Margaret gasped at the way the child suddenly became thin and feverish-looking under the woman's gaze.

"Have you got a clean towel?"

"What for?" demanded Margaret. "Whose baby is it, anyway? Whose room? Whose towel?"

"I want to lie her down and have a look at her. Did you *plan* to have this child, dear?"

"I'll put some newspaper on the bed."

"But that's *dirty* newspaper! Really, this place is very squalid, Mrs. Lenham, if you don't mind my saying so."

"Well, you see, I was going to have an abortion, only—"

"So why didn't you?"

The clinic woman laid her own coat on the bed and put Dorothy Two on it. She poked a finger at the big red raw patches on her thighs.

"Urine burns," she pronounced; and soon Dorothy Two was taken off into care.

Into care—yes, that was what they called it, care. But who cared? It made her howl with bitterness when she was alone in the weeks that followed, and it made her grit her teeth as she strode through the streets looking for revenge, or for her baby, or for Dorothy, not too sure what she was looking for but usually coming home with nothing better than a bag of old tins.

She phoned a lot of numbers—for London seemed suddenly full of numbers to phone if you wanted help. As well as the numbers to phone if you wanted an abortion or if you didn't, there were numbers for if you felt like committing suicide, were going bald, wanted a job, had been arrested or wanted today's recipe. Margaret tried them all, but none of them had any help for her.

Because there was no help for her. In between bouts of crying and phoning, she knew that. She was bereaved of two
daughters. She wished neither of them had ever been born. "I
should have had abortions both times," she muttered.

But you couldn't really say that. Dorothy One had died for
something she believed in (though Margaret was not quite
sure what it was), but she'd have helped keep Dorothy Two if
she'd lived.

First Born is the story of a failed abortion that survives. With an animal's perfect instincts, the abortion seeks out its mother for succor and comfort. *First Born* is also the story of the love-starved mother who embraces the helpless deformato with an almost perverse passion.

The novel's blatant imagery is that of a horror novel, but I like to think of it more as a twisted autobiography with a Gothic veneer. The autobiographical aspects are, of course, metaphorical. Nothing delighted me more than to come up with the image of an abortion as the ultimate outsider.

From the outset, I studiously refused to address the possible political implications of this image. I still refuse to address them, but am happy to offer the following excerpt in the wounded and angry and gleeful spirit in which it was written.

— CAROLINE THOMPSON

First Born

Caroline Thompson

THURSDAY, JULY 19, 1973

AFTER EDWARD WENT, I VOMITED. I THREW UP FOUR times before leaving for the clinic.

Edward had dawdled. He hung around and hung around. He hates taking the bus, but this was only the second time he'd had to. On his way out the door, he kissed me, pressing against me. Pulling back, he pouted. "I don't want to go to work. I want to stay home and play with these." He cupped his hands under my breasts. Fondling them, he pretended to salivate. We both laughed. I was afraid my laugh sounded as forced and phony as it felt.

Toby called while I was getting my things together. He said he woke up with the feeling that I wasn't okay, that something was wrong. He has no idea how right he was. I tried to reassure him. Sweet Toby. He didn't even call the office. Somehow he knew I'd be home. I told him what I'd told Edward—that there was a conference in Virginia that I had to go to for my boss; it didn't start until ten, only now I'd better run because if I didn't I might be late. He was reluctant to let me hang up. He wondered if everything was going all right with Edward. I said yes, everything's fine. It hurt to talk to him. I wanted to tell him what I was going to do. If I could tell anybody, it would be Toby. But I couldn't. What if someday he told Edward? There were people protesting outside the clinic.* Middle-aged women. A few old men. I didn't take a very close look. They were carrying signs: "ABORTION IS MURDER." "SAVE OUR CHILDREN." They began hissing. I hurried. I covered my face, and when I left, it was through a back door. "Don't do it!" one old man croaked. "Spare yourself!" What does an old man know about having babies?

They'd pulled the shades in the waiting room so we couldn't see the people. But we could hear them. Even over the radio. Over that girl's hysterics. She started in with stories she'd read: fetuses left to die in closets, shriveling up because no one would help them, surviving for hours and hours. Spit collected on her lips. Her stringy hair covered her face. Like everybody else, I felt sorry for her. She kept describing one picture she'd seen— a dead baby, blood pouring out of its mouth, its skin hanging on it like old clothes.

Outside, they were chanting.

The three men in the room with us tried to hide their embarrassment in the magazines they straddled across their laps. The four other women and I looked at each other, our eyes meeting unabashedly—seeking what I can't quite say: consolation, companionship, a weird kind of absolution. That's the way I imagine it feels to be in a war together. The girl talked and talked, but no one could understand what she was saying anymore.

An older woman named Beth—we all wore name tags— clicked open her handbag. "Anybody want a mint?" she asked, so casually we might have been in a theater lobby waiting for the play to begin.

*The Rockville Family Planning Associates Medical Group.

She passed the pack around. Mine weren't the only hands that were shaking. But there was nothing we could do for each other.

The counselor who led our group discussion and the clinic receptionist took the weeping girl away. They had to support her. She could barely stand on her own. She resisted at first, overcome by some new terror, then gave in, still whimpering. She couldn't have been more than sixteen years old. She'd also come alone—she and Beth and I. We had nobody's hands to hold. She kept cradling her arms as if there were a baby already in them.

When it was Beth's turn to go, she bit her lip and crossed her fingers. "Wish me luck!" she said loudly, jovially, almost shouting, before jogging out of the room after the nurse. She'd gotten pregnant, she told the group, because she thought she'd reached menopause and had stopped using birth control. She seemed completely unafraid. I even heard her laugh—a distant guffaw from one of the back rooms.

She was the giggler, the girl the screamer, and those of us left were equally divided between the palefaces and the I-don't-give-a-damns. They gave us questionnaires to fill out and two cups for urine samples. They tested my blood, took my temperature, checked my blood pressure.

Instead of shaving my crotch, they sprayed it orange with some freezing disinfectant. When I saw the size of the syringe with the Novocaine in it, I thought I was going to faint. But the shot didn't hurt—just as they'd said it wouldn't. Dr. Strauss narrated the journey describing step after step, an endless monologue, from the examination to clamping on the tenaculum to dilating the cervix with the rods. He chattered through everything, even the worst cramps. The suction from the two-bottled machine pulled and pulled at my insides, and the sweat oozed from my hands, my arms, from between my breasts, like grease on a cooking chicken. The nurse, the same Sally, patted me dry with a cloth.

I gritted my teeth, chewing on the pain. The machine sounded exactly like a vacuum cleaner. The mouth of the tube inside of me sucked and sucked, drawing blood from my ears, my brain, my neck, my shoulders, pulling my hair by the roots from the inside out. It was ghastly and graphic, like the hose had something caught in it. God, the pain. I was screaming and Dr. Strauss sounded worried. "Hang on, Claire," he said. "It'll be over in a second. Hang in there."

Suddenly it all stopped. I heard the machine still whirring. My entire body was soaked with sweat. My clothes were plastered to me. My hair was dripping.

They made me sit up. Sally gave me smelling salts. Dr. Strauss stood between me and the machine, playing with his mustache and looking sorrowfully at me. Sally stretched out her arms to help me down, but just as she did so, she gasped and clapped one of her hands to her mouth. She was gaping at the machine. I looked around the doctor.

There it was—a perfect, tiny, miniature baby. It was still floating in its bubble. Floating peacefully. I could have fit it in the palm of my hand. It was so young it still had a little bit of a tail sticking out from its spine. And its head was huge compared to the rest of its body. It had the first soft tissue folds of genitals, joining and swelling to make a scrotum—a boy. I could see through his skin. There was a pattern of veins underneath. The cord kept sucking at the side of the sac, expecting nourishment. He looked like a moon baby. His arms and legs had no bones, no joints. They were like rubber. His hands floated on either side of his head. His fingers were still webbed. He had the beginnings of fingernails—membrane clinging to each fingertip. He had a nose, nostrils, ears, a slit for a mouth, and eyes.

His eyes appeared closed, the eyelids an unbroken skin, solid but translucent, with the retina showing through from the other side, dark and round and wet. The color was awful, a coating of exaggerated orange-red.

Dr. Strauss reached into the bottle. He picked up the sac. It looked like jelly in his hands. He turned it to see inside from every angle. The eye spots moved, looking for something, sliding from shape to shape, from light to dark to shadow, until they found me.

Dr. Strauss's attitude changed visibly, fascination became panic. He began squeezing the bubble. It shifted, evading him.

I tried to yell.

The bubble bulged, first at one end, then at the other, then in the middle, moving away from wherever he planted his hands. Frustration made him attack it all the more, but he couldn't get his hands around it. The head inside lolled back and forth. The bubble slipped from his hold and dropped to the floor. It seemed to fall forever. When it hit, it bounced. It didn't break. I think I was screaming. Sally stood beside me, paralyzed. Dr. Strauss plunged to the floor after the sac. It rolled uncertainly. Dr. Strauss chased it on his hands and knees.

Groaning, I got to my feet. But Sally was already ahead of me. She scooped the sac up in her hands. Dr. Strauss lunged for her. The sac flew from her hands. Dr. Strauss caught it, cupped it to him like a football, and ran from the room. I heard his footsteps pounding down the hall, fainter and fainter.

They gave me a shot, and when I woke up I was strapped to a bed in a recovery room at the back of the clinic.

From
Zami:
A New Spelling of My Name
Audre Lorde

THE GIRL IN THE LABOR YOUTH LEAGUE WHO HAD
introduced me to Peter had had an abortion, but it had cost
three hundred dollars. The guy had paid for it. I did not have
three hundred dollars, and I had no way of getting three hundred dollars, and I swore her to secrecy telling her the baby
wasn't Peter's. Whatever was going to be done I had to do.
And fast.

Castor oil and a dozen bromo quinine pills didn't help.

Mustard baths gave me a rash, but didn't help either.

Neither did jumping off a table in an empty classroom at
Hunter, and I almost broke my glasses.

Ann was a licensed practical nurse I knew from working
the evening shift at Beth David Hospital. We used to flirt in
the nurses' pantry after midnight when the head nurse was
sneaking a doze in some vacant private room on the floor.
Ann's husband was a soldier in Korea. She was thirty-one
years old—and *knew her way around,* in her own words—
beautiful and friendly, small, sturdy, and deeply Black. One
night, while we were warming the alcohol and talcum for
P.M. care backrubs, she pulled out her right breast to show me
the dark mole which grew at the very line where her deep-

purple aureola met the lighter chocolate brown of her skin, and which, she told me with a mellow laugh, "drove all the doctors crazy."

Ann had introduced me to amphetamine samples on those long sleepy night shifts, and we crashed afterward at her bright kitchenette apartment on Cathedral Parkway, drinking black coffee and gossiping until dawn about the strange habits of head nurses, among other things.

I called Ann at the hospital and met her after work one night. I told her I was pregnant.

"I thought you was gay!"

I heard the disappointed half-question in Ann's voice, and remembered suddenly our little scene in the nurses' pantry. But my experience with people who tried to label me was that they usually did it to either dismiss me or use me. I hadn't even acknowledged my own sexuality yet, much less made any choices about it. I let the remark lay where Jesus flang it.

I asked Ann to get me some ergotrate from the pharmacy, a drug which I had heard from nurses' talk could be used to encourage bleeding.

"Are you crazy?" she said in horror. "You can't mess around with that stuff, girl; it could kill you. It causes hemorrhaging. Let me see what I can find out for you."

Everybody knows somebody, Ann said. For her, it was the mother of another nurse in surgery. Very safe and clean, foolproof and cheap, she said. An induced miscarriage by Foley catheter. A homemade abortion. The narrow hard-rubber tube, used in post-operative cases to keep various body canals open, softened when sterilized. When passed through the cervix into the uterus while soft, it coiled, all fifteen inches, neatly into the womb. Once hardened, its angular turns ruptured the bloody lining and began the uterine contractions that eventually expelled the implanted fetus, along with the membrane. If it wasn't expelled too soon. If it did not also puncture the uterus.

The process took about fifteen hours and cost forty dollars, which was a week and a half's pay.

I walked over to Mrs. Muñoz' apartment after I had finished work at Dr. Sutter's office that afternoon. The January thaw was past, and even though it was only 1:00 p.m., the sun had no warmth. The winter grey of mid-February and the darker patches of dirty Upper-East-Side snow. Against my peacoat in the wind I carried a bag containing the fresh pair of rubber gloves and the new bright-red catheter Ann had taken from the hospital for me, and a sanitary pad. I had most of the contents of my last pay envelope, plus the five dollars Ann had lent me.

"Darling, take off your skirt and panties now while I boil this." Mrs. Muñoz took the catheter from the bag and poured boiling water from a kettle over it and into a shallow basin. I sat curled around myself on the edge of her broad bed, embarrassed by my half-nakedness before this stranger. She pulled on the thin rubber gloves, and setting the basin upon the table, looked over to where I was perched in the corner of the neat, shabby room.

"Lie down, lie down. You scared, huh?" She eyed me from under the clean white kerchief that completely covered her small head. I could not see her hair, and could not tell from her sharp-featured, bright-eyed face how old she was, but she looked so young it surprised me that she could have a daughter old enough to be a nurse.

"You scared? Don't be scared, sweetheart," she said, pick-

117

ing up the basin with the edge of a towel and moving it onto the other edge of the bed.

"Now just lie back and put your legs up. Nothing to be scared of. Nothing to it—I would do it on my own daughter. Now if you was three, four months, say, it would be harder because it would take longer, see? But you not far gone. Don't worry. Tonight, tomorrow, maybe, you hurt a little bit, like bad cramps. You get cramps?"

I nodded, mute, my teeth clenched against the pain. But her hands were busy between my legs as she looked intently at what she was doing.

"You take some aspirin, a little drink. Not too much though. When it's ready, the tube comes back down and the bleeding comes with it. Then, no more baby. Next time you take better care of yourself, darling."

By the time Mrs. Muñoz was finished talking she had skillfully passed the long slender catheter through my cervix into my uterus. The pain had been acute but short. It lay coiled inside of me like a cruel benefactor, soon to rupture the delicate lining and wash away my worries in blood.

Since to me all pain was beyond bearing, even this short bout seemed interminable.

"You see, now, that's all there is to it. That wasn't so bad, was it?" She patted my shuddering thigh reassuringly. "All over. Now get dressed. And wear the pad," she cautioned, as she pulled off the rubber gloves. "You start bleeding in a couple of hours, then you lie down. Here, you want the gloves back?"

I shook my head, and handed her the money. She thanked me. "That's a special price because you a friend of Anna's," she smiled, helping me on with my coat. "By this time tomorrow, it will be all over. If you have any trouble you call me. But no trouble, just a little cramps."

I stopped off on West 4th Street and bought a bottle of apricot brandy for eighty-nine cents. It was the day before my eighteenth birthday and I decided to celebrate my relief. Now all I had to do was hurt.

On the slow Saturday local back to my furnished room in Brighton Beach the cramps began, steadily increasing. Everything's going to be all right now, I kept saying to myself as I leaned over slightly on the subway seat, if I can just get through the next day. I can do it. She said it was safe. The worst is over, and if anything goes wrong I can always go to the hospital. I'll tell them I don't know her name, and I was blindfolded so I couldn't know where I was.

I wondered how bad the pain was going to get, and that terrified me more than anything else. I did not think about how I could die from hemorrhage, or a perforated uterus. The terror was only about the pain.

The subway car was almost empty.

Just last spring around that same time one Saturday morning, I woke up in my mother's house to the smell of bacon frying in the kitchen, and the abrupt realization as I opened my eyes that the dream I had been having of giving birth to a baby girl was in fact only a dream. I sat bolt upright in my bed, facing the little window onto the air shaft, and cried and cried and cried from disappointment until my mother came into the room to see what was wrong.

The train came up out of the tunnel over the bleak edge of south Brooklyn. The Coney Island parachute jump steeple and a huge grey gas storage tank were the only breaks in the leaden skyline.

I dared myself to feel any regrets.

That night about 8 P.M., I was lying curled tightly on my bed, trying to distract myself from the stabbing pains in my groin by deciding whether or not I wanted to dye my hair coal black.

I couldn't begin to think about the risks I was running. But another piece of me was being amazed at my own daring. I had done it. Even more than my leaving home, this action which was tearing my guts apart and from which I could die except I wasn't going to—this action was a kind of shift from safety toward self-preservation. It was a choice of pains. That's what living was all about. I clung to that and tried to feel only proud.

I had not given in. I had not been merely the eye on the ceiling until it was too late. They hadn't gotten me.

There was a tap on the alley door, and I looked out the window. My friend Blossom from school had gotten one of our old high school teachers to drive her out to see if I was "okay," and to bring me a bottle of peach brandy for my birthday. She was one of the people I had consulted, and she had wanted to have nothing to do with an abortion, saying I should have the baby. I didn't bother to tell her Black babies were not adopted. They were absorbed into families, abandoned, or "given up." But not adopted. Nonetheless I knew she was worried to have come all the way from Queens to Manhattan and then to Brighton Beach.

I was touched.

We only talked about inconsequential things. Never a word about what was going on inside of me. Now it was my secret; the only way I could handle it was alone. I sensed they were both grateful that I did.

"You sure you're going to be okay?" Bloss asked. I nodded.

Miss Burman suggested we go for a walk along the board-walk in the crisp February darkness. There was no moon. The walk helped a little, and so did the brandy. But when we got back to my room, I couldn't concentrate on their conversation any more. I was too distracted by the rage gnawing at my belly.

"Do you want us to go?" Bloss asked with her characteristic bluntness. Miss Burman, sympathetic but austere, stood quietly in the doorway looking at my posters. I nodded at Bloss gratefully. Miss Burman lent me five dollars before she left.

The rest of the night was an agony of padding back and forth along the length of the hallway from my bedroom to the bathroom, doubled over in pain, watching clots of blood fall out of my body into the toilet and wondering if I was all right, after all. I had never seen such huge red blobs come from me before. They scared me. I was afraid I might be bleeding to death in that community bathroom in Brighton Beach in the middle of the night of my eighteenth birthday, with a crazy old lady down the hall muttering restlessly in her sleep. But I was going to be all right. Soon this was all going to be over, and I would be safe.

I watched one greyish mucous shape disappear in the bowl, wondering if that was the embryo.

By dawn, when I went to take some more aspirin, the catheter had worked its way out of my body. I was bleeding heavily, very heavily. But my experience in the OB wards told me that I was not hemorrhaging.

I washed the long stiff catheter and laid it away in a drawer, after examining it carefully. This implement of my salvation was a wicked red, but otherwise innocuous-looking.

I took an amphetamine in the thin morning sun and wondered if I should spend a quarter on some coffee and a danish.

I remembered I was supposed to usher at a Hunter College concert that same afternoon, for which I was to be paid ten dollars, a large sum for an afternoon's work, and one that would enable me to repay my debts to Ann and Miss Burman.

I made myself some sweet milky coffee and took a hot bath, even though I was bleeding. After that, the pain dimmed gradually to a dull knocking gripe.

On a sudden whim, I got up and threw on some clothes and went out into the morning. I took the bus into Coney Island to an early-morning foodshop near Nathan's, and had myself a huge birthday breakfast, complete with french fries and an english muffin. I hadn't had a regular meal in a restaurant for a long time. It cost almost half of Miss Burman's five dollars, because it was kosher and expensive. And delicious.

Afterward, I returned home. I lay resting upon my bed, filled with a sense of well-being and relief from pain and terror that was almost euphoric. I really was all right.

As the morning slipped into afternoon, I realized that I was exhausted. But the thought of making ten dollars for one afternoon's work got me wearily up and back onto the weekend local train for the long trip to Hunter College.

By mid-afternoon my legs were quivering. I walked up and down the aisles dully, hardly hearing the string quartet. In the last part of the concert, I went into the ladies room to change my tampax and the pads I was wearing. In the stall, I was seized by a sudden wave of nausea that bent me double, and I promptly and with great force lost my $2.50-with-tip Coney Island breakfast, which I had never digested. Weakened and shivering, I sat on the stool, my head against the wall. A fit of renewed cramps swept through me so sharply that I moaned softly.

Miz Lewis, the Black ladies-room attendant who had known me from the bathrooms of Hunter High School, was in the back of the room in her cubby, and she had seen me come into the otherwise empty washroom.

"Is that you, Autray, moaning like that? You all right?" I saw her low-shoed feet stop outside my stall.

"Yes ma'am," I gasped through the door, cursing my luck to have walked into that particular bathroom. "It's just my period."

I steadied myself, and arranged my clothes. When I finally stepped out, bravely and with my head high, Miz Lewis was still standing outside, her arms folded.

She had always maintained a steady but impersonal interest in the lives of the few Black girls at the high school, and she was a familiar face which I was glad to see when I met her in the washroom of the college in the autumn. I told her I was going to the college now, and that I had left home. Miz Lewis had raised her eyebrows and pursed her lips, shaking her grey head. "You girls sure are somethin'!" she'd said.

In the uncompromising harshness of the fluorescent lights, Miz Lewis gazed at me intently through her proper gold spectacles, which perched upon her broad brown nose like round antennae.

"Girl, you sure you all right? Don't sound all right to me." She peered up into my face. "Sit down here a minute. You just started? You white like some other people's child."

I took her seat, gratefully. "I'm all right, Miz Lewis," I protested. "I just have bad cramps, that's all."

"Jus' cramps? That bad? Then why you come here like that today for? You ought to be home in bed, the way your eyes looking. You want some coffee, honey?" She offered me her cup.

"Cause I need the money, Miz Lewis. I'll be all right; I really will." I shook my head to the coffee, and stood up. Another cramp slid up from my clenched thighs and rammed into the small of my back, but I only rested my head against the edge of the stalls. Then, taking a paper towel from the stack on the glass shelf in front of me, I wet it and wiped the cold sweat from my forehead. I wiped the rest of my face, and blotted my faded lipstick carefully. I grinned at my reflection in the mirror and at Miz Lewis standing to the side behind me, her arms still folded against her broad short-waisted bosom. She sucked her teeth with a sharp intake of breath and sighed a long sigh.

"Chile, why don't you go on back home to your mama, where you belong?"

I almost burst into tears. I felt like screaming, drowning out her plaintive, kindly, old-woman's voice that kept pretending everything was so simple.

"Don't you think she's worrying about you? Do she know you in all this trouble?"

"I'm not in trouble, Miz Lewis. I just don't feel well because of my period." Turning away, I crumpled up the used towel and dropped it into the basket, and then sat down again, heavily. My legs were shockingly weak.

"Yeah. Well." Miz Lewis sucked her teeth again, and put her hand into her apron pocket. "Here," she said, pulling four dollars out of her purse. "You take these and get yourself a taxi home." She knew I lived in Brooklyn. "And you go right home, now. I'll cross your name off the list downstairs for you. And you can pay me back when you get it."

I took the crumpled bills from her dark, work-wise hands. "Thanks a lot, Miz Lewis," I said gratefully. I stood up again, this time a little more steadily. "But don't you worry about me, this won't last very long." I walked shakily to the door.

"And you put your feet up, and a cold compress on your tummy, and you stay in bed for a few days, too," she called after me, as I made my way to the elevators to the main floor.

I asked the cab to take me around to the alley entrance, instead of getting out on Brighton Beach Avenue. I was afraid my legs might not take me where I wanted to go. I wondered if I had almost fainted.

Once indoors, I took three aspirins and slept for twenty-four hours.

When I awoke Monday afternoon, the bed-sheets were stained, but my bleeding had slowed to normal and the cramps were gone.

I wondered if I had gotten some bad food at the foodshop Sunday morning that had made me sick. Usually I never got upset stomachs, and prided myself on my cast-iron digestion. The following day I went back to school.

On Friday, after classes, before I went to work, I picked up my money for ushering. I sought out Miz Lewis in the auditorium washroom and paid her back her four dollars.

"Oh, thank you, Autray," she said, looking a little surprised. She folded the bills up neatly and tucked them back into the green snap-purse she kept in her uniform apron pocket. "How you feeling?"

"Fine, Miz Lewis," I said jauntily. "I told you I was going to be all right."

"You did not! You said you *was* all right and I knew you wasn't, so don't tell me none of that stuff, I don't want to hear." Miz Lewis eyed me balefully.

"You gon' back home to your mama, yet?"

From

The Women of Brewster Place

Gloria Naylor

LUCIELIA LOUISE TURNER

THE SUNLIGHT WAS STILL WATERY AS BEN TRUDGED
into Brewster Place, and the street had just begun to yawn and
stretch itself. He eased himself onto his garbage can, which
was pushed against the sagging brick wall that turned Brewster into a dead-end street. The metallic cold of the can's lid
seeped into the bottom of his thin trousers. Sucking on a piece
of breakfast sausage caught in his back teeth, he began to
muse. Mighty cold, these spring mornings. The old days you
could build a good trash fire in one of them barrels to keep
warm. Well, don't want no summons now, and can't freeze to
death. Yup, can't freeze to death.

His daily soliloquy completed, he reached into his coat pocket
and pulled out a crumpled brown bag that contained his morning sun. The cheap red liquid moved slowly down his throat,
providing immediate justification as the blood began to warm in
his body. In the hazy light a lean dark figure began to make its
way slowly up the block. It hesitated in front of the stoop at 316,
but looking around and seeing Ben, it hurried over.

"Yo, Ben."

"Hey, Eugene, I thought that was you. Ain't seen ya round
for a coupla days."

"Yeah." The young man put his hands in his pockets, frowned into the ground, and kicked the edge of Ben's can. "The funeral's today, ya know."

"Yeah."

"You going?" He looked up into Ben's face.

"Naw, I ain't got no clothes for them things. Can't abide 'em no way—too sad—it being a baby and all."

"Yeah. I was going myself, people expect it, ya know?"

"Yeah."

"But, man, the way Ciel's friends look at me and all—like I was filth or something. Hey, I even tried to go see Ciel in the hospital, heard she was freaked out and all."

"Yeah, she took it real bad."

"Yeah, well, damn, I took it bad. It was my kid, too, ya know. But Mattie, that fat, black bitch, just standin' in the hospital hall sayin' to me—to me, now, 'Whatcha want?' Like I was a fuckin' germ or something. Man, I just turned and left. You gotta be treated with respect, ya know?"

"Yeah."

"I mean, I should be there today with my woman in the limo and all, sittin' up there, doin' it right. But how you gonna be a man with them ball-busters tellin' everybody it was my fault and I should be the one dead? Damn!"

"Yeah, a man's gotta be a man." Ben felt the need to wet his reply with another sip. "Have some?"

"Naw, I'm gonna be heading on—Ciel don't need me today. I bet that frig, Mattie, rides in the head limo, wearing the pants. Shit—let 'em." He looked up again. "Ya know?"

"Yup."

"Take it easy, Ben." He turned to go.

"You too, Eugene."

"Hey, you going?"

"Naw."

"Me neither. Later."

"Later, Eugene."

Funny, Ben thought, Eugene ain't stopped to chat like that for a long time—near on a year, yup, a good year. He took another swallow to help him bring back the year-old conversation, but it didn't work; the second and third one didn't either. But he did remember that it had been an early spring morning like this one, and Eugene had been wearing those same tight jeans. He had hesitated outside of 316 then, too. But that time he went in...

Lucielia had just run water into the tea kettle and was putting it on the burner when she heard the cylinder turn. He didn't have to knock on the door; his key still fit the lock. Her thin knuckles gripped the handle of the kettle, but she didn't turn around. She knew. The last eleven months of her life hung compressed in the air between the click of the lock and his "Yo, baby."

The vibrations from those words rode like parasites on the air waves and came rushing into her kitchen, smashing the compression into indistinguishable days and hours that swirled dizzily before her. It was all there: the frustration of being left alone, sick, with a month-old baby; her humiliation reflected in the caseworker's blue eyes for the unanswerable "you can find him to have it, but can't find him to take care of it" smile; the raw urges that crept, uninvited, between her thighs on countless nights; the eternal whys all meshed with the explainable hate and unexplainable love. They kept circling in such a confusing pattern before her that she couldn't seem to grab even one to answer him with. So there was nothing in Lucielia's face when she turned it toward Eugene, standing in her kitchen door holding a ridiculously pink Easter bunny, nothing but sheer relief....

"So he's back." Mattie sat at Lucielia's kitchen table, playing with Serena. It was rare that Mattie ever spoke more than two sentences to anybody about anything. She didn't have to. She chose her words with the grinding precision of a diamond cutter's drill.

"You think I'm a fool, don't you?"

"I ain't said that."

"You didn't have to," Ciel snapped.

"Why you mad at me, Ciel? It's your life, honey."

"Oh, Mattie, you don't understand. He's really straightened up this time. He's got a new job on the docks that pays real good, and he was just so depressed before with the new baby and no work. You'll see. He's even gone out now to buy paint and stuff to fix up the apartment. And, and Serena needs a daddy."

"You ain't gotta convince me, Ciel."

No, she wasn't talking to Mattie, she was talking to herself. She was convincing herself it was the new job and the paint and Serena that let him back into her life. Yet, the real truth went beyond her scope of understanding. When she laid her head in the hollow of his neck there was a deep musky scent to his body that brought back the ghosts of the Tennessee soil of her childhood. It reached up and lined the inside of her nostrils so that she inhaled his presence almost every minute of her life. The feel of his sooty flesh penetrated the skin of her fingers and coursed through her blood and became one, somewhere, wherever it was, with her actual being. But how do you tell yourself, let alone this practical old woman who loves you, that he was back because of that. So you don't.

You get up and fix you both another cup of coffee, calm the fretting baby on your lap with her pacifier, and you pray silently— very silently—behind veiled eyes that the man will stay.

Ciel was trying to remember exactly when it had started to go wrong again. Her mind sought for the slender threads of a clue that she could trace back to—perhaps—something she had said or done. Her brow was set tightly in concentration as she folded towels and smoothed the wrinkles over and over, as if the answer lay concealed in the stubborn creases of the terry cloth.

The months since Eugene's return began to tick off slowly before her, and she examined each one to pinpoint when the nagging whispers of trouble had begun in her brain. The friction on the towels increased when she came to the month that she had gotten pregnant again, but it couldn't be that. Things were different now. She wasn't sick as she had been with Serena, he was still working—no it wasn't the baby. It's not the baby, it's not the baby—the rhythm of those words sped up the motion of her hands, and she had almost yanked and folded and pressed them into a reality when, bewildered, she realized that she had run out of towels.

Ciel jumped when the front door slammed shut. She waited tensely for the metallic bang of his keys on the coffee table and the blast of the stereo. Lately that was how Eugene announced his presence home. Ciel walked into the living room with the motion of a swimmer entering a cold lake.

"Eugene, you're home early, huh?"

"You see anybody else sittin' here?" He spoke without looking at her and rose to turn up the stereo.

He wants to pick a fight, she thought, confused and hurt. He knows Serena's taking her nap, and now I'm supposed to say, Eugene, the baby's asleep, please cut the music down. Then he's going to say, you mean a man can't even relax in his own home without being picked on? I'm not picking on you, but you're going to wake up the baby. Which is always supposed to lead to: You don't give a damn about me. Everybody's more important than me—that kid, your friends, everybody. I'm just chickenshit around here, huh?

All this went through Ciel's head as she watched him leave the stereo and drop defiantly back down on the couch. Without saying a word, she turned and went into the bedroom. She looked down on the peaceful face of her daughter and softly caressed her small cheek. Her heart became full as she realized, this is the only thing I have ever loved without pain. She pulled the sheet gently over the tiny shoulders and firmly closed the door, protecting her from the music. She then went into the kitchen and began washing the rice for their dinner.

Eugene, seeing that he had been left alone, turned off the stereo and came and stood in the kitchen door.

"I lost my job today," he shot at her, as if she had been the cause.

The water was turning cloudy in the rice pot, and the force of the stream from the faucet caused scummy bubbles to rise to the surface. These broke and sprayed tiny starchy particles onto the dirty surface. Each bubble that broke seemed to increase the volume of the dogged whispers she had been ignoring for the last few months. She poured the dirty water off the rice to destroy and silence them, then watched with a malicious joy as they disappeared down the drain.

"So now, how in the hell I'm gonna make it with no money, huh? And another brat comin' here, huh?"

The second change of the water was slightly clearer, but the starch-speckled bubbles were still there, and this time there was no way to pretend deafness to their message. She had stood at that sink countless times before, washing rice, and she knew the water was never going to be totally clear. She couldn't stand there forever—her fingers were getting cold, and the rest of the dinner had to be fixed, and Serena would be waking up soon and wanting attention. Feverishly she poured the water off and tried again.

"I'm fuckin' sick of never getting ahead. Babies and bills, that's all you good for."

The bubbles were almost transparent now, but when they broke they left light trails of starch on top of the water that curled around her fingers. She knew it would be useless to try again. Defeated, Ciel placed the wet pot on the burner, and the flames leaped up bright red and orange, turning the water droplets clinging on the outside into steam.

Turning to him, she silently acquiesced. "All right, Eugene, what do you want me to do?"

He wasn't going to let her off so easily. "Hey, baby, look, I don't care what you do. I just can't have all these hassles on me right now, ya know?"

"I'll get a job. I don't mind, but I've got no one to keep Serena, and you don't want Mattie watching her."

"Mattie—no way. That fat bitch'll turn the kid against me. She hates my ass, and you know it."

"No, she doesn't, Eugene." Ciel remembered throwing that at Mattie once. "You hate him, don't you?" "Naw, honey," and she had cupped both hands on Ciel's face. "Maybe I just loves you too much."

"I don't give a damn what you say—she ain't minding my kid."

"Well, look, after the baby comes, they can tie my tubes—I don't care." She swallowed hard to keep down the lie.

"And what the hell we gonna feed it when it gets here, huh—air? With two kids and you on my back, I ain't never gonna have nothin'." He came and grabbed her by the shoulders and was shouting into her face. "Nothin', do you hear me, nothin'!"

"Nothing to it, Mrs. Turner." The face over hers was as calm and antiseptic as the room she lay in. "Please, relax. I'm going to give you a local anesthetic and then perform a simple D&C, or what you'd call a scraping to clean out the uterus. Then you'll rest here for about an hour and be on your way. There won't even be much bleeding." The voice droned on in its practiced monologue, peppered with sterile kindness.

Ciel was not listening. It was important that she keep herself completely isolated from these surroundings. All the activities of the past week of her life were balled up and jammed on the right side of her brain, as if belonging to some other woman. And when she had endured this one last thing for her, she would push it up there, too, and then one day give it all to her—Ciel wanted no part of it.

The next few days Ciel found it difficult to connect herself up again with her own world. Everything seemed to have taken on new textures and colors. When she washed the dishes, the plates felt peculiar in her hands, and she was more conscious of their smoothness and the heat of the water. There was a disturbing split second between someone talking to her and the words penetrating sufficiently to elicit a response. Her neighbors left her presence with slight frowns of puzzlement, and Eugene could be heard mumbling, "Moody bitch."

She became terribly possessive of Serena. She refused to leave her alone, even with Eugene. The little girl went everywhere with Ciel, toddling along on plump uncertain legs. When someone asked to hold or play with her, Ciel sat nearby, watching every move. She found herself walking into the bedroom several times when the child napped to see if she was still breathing. Each time she chided herself for this unreasonable foolishness, but within the next few minutes some strange force still drove her back.

Spring was slowly beginning to announce itself at Brewster Place. The arthritic cold was seeping out of the worn gray bricks, and the tenants with apartment windows facing the street were awakened by six o'clock sunlight. The music no longer blasted inside of 3C, and Ciel grew strong with the peacefulness of her household. The playful laughter of her daughter, heard more often now, brought a sort of redemption with it.

"Isn't she marvelous, Mattie? You know she's even trying to make whole sentences. Come on, baby, talk for Auntie Mattie."

Serena, totally uninterested in living up to her mother's proud claims, was trying to tear a gold-toned button off the bosom of Mattie's dress.

"It's so cute. She even knows her father's name. She says, my da da is Gene."

"Better teach her your name," Mattie said, while playing with the baby's hand. "She'll be using it more."

Ciel's mouth flew open to ask her what she meant by that, but she checked herself. It was useless to argue with Mattie. You could take her words however you wanted. The burden of their truth lay with you, not her.

Eugene came through the front door and stopped short when he saw Mattie. He avoided being around her as much as possible. She was always polite to him, but he sensed a silent condemnation behind even her most innocent words. He constantly felt the need to prove himself in front of her. These frustrations often took the form of unwarranted rudeness on his part.

Serena struggled out of Mattie's lap and went toward her father and tugged on his legs to be picked up. Ignoring the child and cutting short the greetings of the two women, he said coldly, "Ciel, I wanna talk to you."

Sensing trouble, Mattie rose to go. "Ciel, why don't you let me take Serena downstairs for a while. I got some ice cream for her."

"She can stay right here," Eugene broke in. "If she needs ice cream, I can buy it for her."

Hastening to soften his abruptness, Ciel said, "That's okay, Mattie, it's almost time for her nap. I'll bring her later—after dinner."

"All right. Now you all keep good." Her voice was warm. "You too, Eugene," she called back from the front door.

The click of the lock restored his balance to him. "Why in the hell is she always up here?"

"You just had your chance—why didn't you ask her yourself? If you don't want her here, tell her to stay out," Ciel snapped back confidently, knowing he never would.

"Look, I ain't got time to argue with you about that old hag.

I got big doings in the making, and I need you to help me pack."
Without waiting for a response, he hurried into the bedroom
and pulled his old leather suitcase from under the bed.

A tight, icy knot formed in the center of Ciel's stomach and
began to melt rapidly, watering the blood in her legs so that
they almost refused to support her weight. She pulled Serena
back from following Eugene and sat her in the middle of the
living room floor.

"Here, honey, play with the blocks for Mommy—she has to
talk to Daddy." She piled a few plastic alphabet blocks in front
of the child, and on her way out of the room, she glanced
around quickly and removed the glass ashtrays off the coffee
table and put them on a shelf over the stereo.

Then, taking a deep breath to calm her racing heart, she
started toward the bedroom.

Serena loved the light colorful cubes and would sometimes sit
for an entire half-hour, repeatedly stacking them up and kicking them over with her feet. The hollow sound of their falling
fascinated her, and she would often bang two of them
together to re-create the magical noise. She was sitting, con-
tentedly engaged in this particular activity, when a slow dark
movement along the baseboard caught her eye.

A round black roach was making its way from behind the
couch toward the kitchen. Serena threw one of her blocks at
the insect, and, feeling the vibrations of the wall above it, the
roach sped around the door into the kitchen. Finding a totally
new game to amuse herself, Serena took off behind the insect
with a block in each hand. Seeing her moving toy trying to
bury itself under the linoleum by the garbage pail she threw
another block, and the frantic roach now raced along the wall

and found security in the electric wall socket under the kitchen table.

Angry at losing her plaything, she banged the block against the socket, attempting to get it to come back out. When that failed, she unsuccessfully tried to poke her chubby finger into the thin horizontal slit. Frustrated, tiring of the game, she sat under the table and realized she had found an entirely new place in the house to play. The shiny chrome of the table and chair legs drew her attention, and she experimented with the sound of the block against their smooth surfaces.

This would have entertained her until Ciel came, but the roach, thinking itself safe, ventured outside of the socket. Serena gave a cry of delight and attempted to catch her lost playmate, but it was too quick and darted back into the wall. She tried once again to poke her finger into the slit. Then a bright slender object, lying dropped and forgotten, came into her view. Picking up the fork, Serena finally managed to fit the thin flattened prongs into the electric socket.

Eugene was avoiding Ciel's eyes as he packed. "You know, baby, this is really a good deal after me bein' out of work for so long." He moved around her still figure to open the drawer that held his T-shirts and shorts. "And hell, Maine ain't far. Once I get settled on the docks up there, I'll be able to come home all the time."

"Why can't you take us with you?" She followed each of his movements with her eyes and saw herself being buried in the case under the growing pile of clothes.

"'Cause I gotta check out what's happening before I drag you and the kid up there."

"I don't mind. We'll make do. I've learned to live on very little."

"No, it just won't work right now. I gotta see my way clear first."

"Eugene, please." She listened with growing horror to herself quietly begging.

"No, and that's it!" He flung his shoes into the suitcase.

"Well, how far is it? Where did you say you were going?" She moved toward the suitcase.

"I told ya—the docks in Newport."

"That's not in Maine. You said you were going to Maine."

"Well, I made a mistake."

"How could you know about a place so far up? Who got you the job?"

"A friend."

"Who?"

"None of your damned business!" His eyes were flashing with the anger of a caged animal. He slammed down the top of the suitcase and yanked it off the bed.

"You're lying, aren't you? You don't have a job, do you? Do you?"

"Look, Ciel, believe whatever the fuck you want to. I gotta go." He tried to push past her.

She grabbed the handle of the case. "No, you can't go."

"Why?"

Her eyes widened slowly. She realized that to answer that would require that she uncurl that week of her life, pushed safely up into her head, when she had done all those terrible things for that other woman who had wanted an abortion. She and she alone would have to take responsibility for them now. He must understand what those actions had meant to her, but somehow, he had meant even more. She sought desperately for the right words, but it all came out as—

"Because I love you."

"Well, that ain't good enough."

Ciel had let the suitcase go before he jerked it away. She looked at Eugene, and the poison of reality began to spread through her body like gangrene. It drew his scent out of her nostrils and scraped the veil from her eyes, and he stood before her just as he really was—a tall, skinny black man with arrogance and selfishness twisting his mouth into a strange shape. And, she thought, I don't feel anything now. But soon, very soon, I will start to hate you. I promise—I will hate you. And I'll never forgive myself for not having done it sooner—soon enough to have saved my baby. Oh, dear God, my baby.

Eugene thought the tears that began to crowd into her eyes were for him. But she was allowing herself this one last luxury of brief mourning for the loss of something denied to her. It troubled her that she wasn't sure exactly what that something was, or which one of them was to blame for taking it away. Ciel began to feel the overpowering need to be near someone who loved her. I'll get Serena and we'll go visit Mattie now, she thought in a daze.

Then they heard the scream from the kitchen.

The church was small and dark. The air hung about them like a stale blanket. Ciel looked straight ahead, oblivious to the seats filling up behind her. She didn't feel the damp pressure of Mattie's heavy arm or the doubt that invaded the air over Eugene's absence. The plaintive Merciful Jesuses, lightly sprinkled with sobs, were lost in her ears. Her dry eyes were locked on the tiny pearl-gray casket, flanked with oversized arrangements of red-carnationed bleeding hearts and white-lilied eternal circles. The sagging chords that came loping out

of the huge organ and mixed with the droning voice of the
black-robed old man behind the coffin were also unable to
penetrate her.

Ciel's whole universe existed in the seven feet of space
between herself and her child's narrow coffin. There was not
even room for this comforting God whose melodious virtues
floated around her sphere, attempting to get in. Obviously, He
had deserted or damned her, it didn't matter which. All Ciel
knew was that her prayers had gone unheeded—that afternoon she had lifted her daughter's body off the kitchen floor,
those blank days in the hospital, and now. So she was left to do
what God had chosen not to.

People had mistaken it for shock when she refused to cry.
They thought it some special sort of grief when she stopped eating and even drinking water unless forced to; her hair went
uncombed and her body unbathed. But Ciel was not grieving
for Serena. She was simply tired of hurting. And she was forced
to slowly give up the life that God had refused to take from her.

After the funeral the well-meaning came to console and offer
their dog-eared faith in the form of coconut cakes, potato pies,
fried chicken, and tears. Ciel sat in the bed with her back
resting against the headboard; her long thin fingers, still
as midnight frost on a frozen pond, lay on the covers. She
acknowledged their kindnesses with nods of her head and
slight lip movements, but no sound. It was as if her voice was
too tired to make the journey from the diaphragm through
the larynx to the mouth.

Her visitors' impotent words flew against the steel edge of
her pain, bled slowly, and returned to die in the senders'
throats. No one came too near. They stood around the door and

the dressing table, or sat on the edges of the two worn chairs that needed upholstering, but they unconsciously pushed themselves back against the wall as if her hurt was contagious.

A neighbor woman entered in studied certainty and stood in the middle of the room. "Child, I know how you feel, but don't do this to yourself. I lost one, too. The Lord will…" And she choked, because the words were jammed down into her throat by the naked force of Ciel's eyes. Ciel had opened them fully now to look at the woman, but raw fires had eaten them worse than lifeless—worse than death. The woman saw in that mute appeal for silence the ragings of a personal hell flowing through Ciel's eyes. And just as she went to reach for the girl's hand, she stopped as if a muscle spasm had overtaken her body and, cowardly, shrank back. Reminiscences of old, dried-over pains were no consolation in the face of this. They had the effect of cold beads of water on a hot iron—they danced and fizzled up while the room stank from their steam.

Mattie stood in the doorway, and an involuntary shudder went through her when she saw Ciel's eyes. Dear God, she thought, she's dying, and right in front of our faces.

"Merciful Father, no!" she bellowed. There was no prayer, no bended knee or sackcloth supplication in those words, but a blasphemous fireball that shot forth and went smashing against the gates of heaven, raging and kicking, demanding to be heard.

"No! No! No!" Like a black Brahman cow, desperate to protect her young, she surged into the room, pushing the neighbor woman and the others out of her way. She approached the bed with her lips clamped shut in such force that the muscles in her jaw and the back of her neck began to ache.

She sat on the edge of the bed and enfolded the tissue-thin

body in her huge ebony arms. And she rocked. Ciel's body was so hot it burned Mattie when she first touched her, but she held on and rocked. Back and forth, back and forth—she had Ciel so tightly she could feel her young breasts flatten against the buttons of her dress. The black mammoth gripped so firmly that the slightest increase of pressure would have cracked the girl's spine. But she rocked.

And somewhere from the bowels of her being came a moan from Ciel, so high at first it couldn't be heard by anyone there, but the yard dogs began an unholy howling. And Mattie rocked. And then, agonizingly slow, it broke its way through the parched lips in a spaghetti-thin column of air that could be faintly heard in the frozen room.

Ciel moaned. Mattie rocked. Propelled by the sound, Mattie rocked her out of that bed, out of that room, into a blue vastness just underneath the sun and above time. She rocked her over Aegean seas so clean they shone like crystal, so clear the fresh blood of sacrificed babies torn from their mother's arms and given to Neptune could be seen like pink froth on the water. She rocked her on and on, past Dachau, where soul-gutted Jewish mothers swept their children's entrails off laboratory floors. They flew past the spilled brains of Senegalese infants whose mothers had dashed them on the wooden sides of slave ships. And she rocked on.

She rocked her into her childhood and let her see murdered dreams. And she rocked her back, back into the womb, to the nadir of her hurt, and they found it—a slight silver splinter, embedded just below the surface of the skin. And Mattie rocked and pulled—and the splinter gave way, but its roots were deep, gigantic, and ragged, and they tore up flesh with bits of fat and muscle tissue clinging to them. They left a huge hole, which was already starting to pus over, but Mattie was satisfied. It would heal.

The bile that had formed a tight knot in Ciel's stomach began to rise and gagged her just as it passed her throat. Mattie put her hand over the girl's mouth and rushed her out the now-empty room to the toilet. Ciel retched yellowish-green phlegm, and she brought up white lumps of slime that hit the seat of the toilet and rolled off, splattering onto the tiles. After a while she heaved only air, but the body did not seem to want to stop. It was exorcising the evilness of pain.

Mattie cupped her hands under the faucet and motioned for Ciel to drink and clean her mouth. When the water left Ciel's mouth, it tasted as if she had been rinsing with a mild acid. Mattie drew a tub of hot water and undressed Ciel. She let the nightgown fall off the narrow shoulders, over the pitifully thin breasts and jutting hipbones. She slowly helped her into the water, and it was like a dried brown autumn leaf hitting the surface of a puddle.

And slowly she bathed her. She took the soap, and, using only her hands, she washed Ciel's hair and the back of her neck. She raised her arms and cleaned the armpits, soaping well the downy brown hair there. She let the soap slip between the girl's breasts, and she washed each one separately, cupping it in her hands. She took each leg and even cleaned under the toenails. Making Ciel rise and kneel in the tub, she cleaned the crack in her behind, soaped her pubic hair, and gently washed the creases in her vagina—slowly, reverently, as if handling a newborn.

She took her from the tub and toweled her in the same manner she had been bathed—as if too much friction would break the skin tissue. All of this had been done without either woman saying a word. Ciel stood there, naked, and felt the cool air play against the clean surface of her skin. She had the sensation of fresh mint coursing through her pores. She closed her eyes and the fire was gone. Her tears no longer fried within her, killing her internal organs with their steam. So Ciel began to cry—there, naked, in the center of the bathroom floor.

Mattie emptied the tub and rinsed it. She led the still-naked Ciel to a chair in the bedroom. The tears were flowing so freely now Ciel couldn't see, and she allowed herself to be led as if blind. She sat on the chair and cried—head erect. Since she made no effort to wipe them away, the tears dripped down her chin and landed on her chest and rolled down to her stomach and onto her dark pubic hair. Ignoring Ciel, Mattie took away the crumpled linen and made the bed, stretching the sheets tight and fresh. She beat the pillows into a virgin plumpness and dressed them in white cases.

And Ciel sat. And cried. The unmolested tears had rolled down her parted thighs and were beginning to wet the chair. But they were cold and good. She put out her tongue and began to drink in their saltiness, feeding on them. The first tears were gone. Her thin shoulders began to quiver, and spasms circled her body as new tears came—this time, hot and stinging. And she sobbed, the first sound she'd made since the moaning.

Mattie took the edges of the dirty sheets she'd pulled off the bed and wiped the mucus that had been running out of Ciel's nose. She then led her freshly wet, glistening body, baptized now, to the bed. She covered her with one sheet and laid a towel across the pillow—it would help for a while.

And Ciel lay down and cried. But Mattie knew the tears would end. And she would sleep. And morning would come.

The Wild Palms

William Faulkner

HE DELIVERED THE BOWL HIMSELF — A SHORTISH
fattish untidy man with linen not quite fresh, sidling a little
clumsily through the oleander hedge with the bowl covered
by a yet-creased (and not yet even laundered, it was that new)
linen napkin, lending an air of awkward kindliness even to
the symbol which he carried of the uncompromising Christian
deed performed not with sincerity or pity but through duty—
and lowered it (she had not risen from the chair nor moved
save the hard cat's eyes) as if the bowl contained nitro-glycerin,
the fattish unshaven mask beaming foolishly but behind the
mask the eyes of the doctor within the Doctor shrewd, miss-
ing nothing, examining without smiling and without diffi-
dence the face of the woman who was not thin but actually
gaunt, thinking *Yes. A degree or two. Perhaps three. But not the
heart* then waking, rousing, to find the blank feral eyes staring
at him, whom to his certain knowledge they could scarcely
have seen before, with profound and illimitable hatred. It was
quite impersonal, as when the person in whom joy already
exists looks out at any post or tree with pleasure and happiness. He (the doctor) was without vanity; it was not at him the
hatred was directed. *It's at the whole human race,* he thought.

Or no, no. Wait. Wait—the veil about to break, the cogs of deduction about to mesh—*Not at the race of mankind but at the race of man, the masculine. But why? Why?* His wife would have noticed the faint mark of the absent wedding ring, but he, the doctor, saw more than that: *She has borne children,* he thought. *One, anyway; I would stake my degree on that. And if Cofer* (he was the agent) *is right about his not being her husband—and he should be, should be able to tell, smell, as he says, since he is apparently in the business of renting beach cottages for the same reason or under the same compulsion, vicarious need, which drives certain people in the cities to equip and supply rooms to clandestine and fictitious names....Say she had come to hate the race of men enough to desert husband and children; good. Yet, to have gone not only to another man, but to live apparently in penury, and herself sick, really sick. Or to have deserted husband and children for another man and poverty, and then to have—to have—to...* He could feel, hear them: the cogs, clicking, going fast; he felt a need for terrific haste in order to keep up, a premonition that the final cog would click and the bell of comprehension ring and he would not be quite near enough to see and hear: *Yes. Yes. What is it that man as a race can have done to her that she would look upon such a manifestation of it as I, whom she has never seen before and would not look at twice if she had, with that same hatred through which he must walk each time he comes up from the beach with an armful of firewood to cook the very food which she eats?*

She did not even offer to take the dish from him. "It's not soup, it's gumbo," he said. "My wife made it. She—we..." She did not move, looking at him as he stooped fatly in his crumpled seersucker, with the careful tray; he did not even hear the man until she spoke to him.

"Thanks," she said. "Take it into the house, Harry." Now she was not even looking at the doctor any more. "Thank your wife," she said.

He was thinking about his two tenants as he descended the stairs behind the jerking pencil of light, into the staling odor of gumbo in the lower hall, toward the door, the knocking. It was from no presentiment, premonition that the knocker was the man named Harry. It was because he had thought of nothing else for four days—this snuffy middleaging man in the archaic sleeping garment now become one of the national props of comedy, roused from slumber in the stale bed of his childless wife and already thinking of (perhaps having been dreaming of) the profound and distracted blaze of objectless hatred in the strange woman's eyes; and he again with that sense of imminence, of being just beyond a veil from something, of groping just without the veil and even touching but not quite, almost seeing but not quite, the shape of truth, so that without being aware of it he stopped dead on the stairs in his old-fashioned list slippers, thinking swiftly: *Yes. Yes. Something which the entire race of men, males, has done to her or she believes has done to her.*

The knocking came again now, as if the knocker had become aware that he had stopped through some alteration of the torch's beam seen beneath the door itself and now began to knock again with that diffident insistence of a stranger seeking aid late at night, and the doctor moved again, not in response to the renewed knocking, who had had no presentiment, but as though the renewal of the knocking had merely coincided with the recurrent old stale impasse of the four days' bafflement and groping, capitulant and recapitulant; as though instinct perhaps moved him again, the body capable of motion, not the intellect, believing that physical advancement might bring him nearer the veil at the instant when it would part and reveal in inviolable isolation that truth which he almost touched. So it was without premonition that he opened the door and peered out, bringing the torch's beam on the knocker. It was the man called Harry. He stood there in the darkness, in the strong steady seawind filled with the dry clashing of invisible palm fronds, as the doctor had always seen him, in the soiled ducks and the sleeveless undershirt, murmuring the conventional amenities about the hour and the need, asking to use the telephone while the doctor, his nightshirt streaming about his flabby calves, peered at the caller and thought in a fierce surge of triumph: *Now I am going to find out what it is.* "Yes," he said, "you wont need the telephone. I am a doctor myself."

"Oh," the other said. "Can you come at once?"

"Yes. Just let me slip on my pants. What's the trouble? So I shall know what to bring."

For an instant the other hesitated; this familiar to the doctor too who had seen it before and believed he knew its source: that innate and ineradicable instinct of mankind to attempt to conceal some of the truth even from the doctor or lawyer for whose skill and knowledge they are paying. "She's bleeding," he said. "What will your fee—"

But the doctor did not notice this. He was talking to himself: *Ah. Yes. Why didn't I...Lungs, of course. Why didn't I think of that?* "Yes," he said. "Will you wait here? Or perhaps inside? I wont be but a minute."

"I'll wait here," the other said. But the doctor did not hear that either. He was already running back up the stairs; he trotted into the bedroom where his wife rose on one elbow in the bed and watched him struggle into his trousers, his shadow, cast by the lamp on the low table by the bed, antic on the wall, her shadow also monstrous, gorgonlike from the rigid paper-wrapped twists of gray hair above the gray face above the high-necked night-dress which also looked gray, as if every garment she owned had partaken of that grim iron-color of her implacable and invincible morality which, the doctor was to realize later, was almost omniscient. "Yes," he said, "bleeding. Probably hemorrhage. Lungs. And why in the world I didn't—"

"More likely he has cut or shot her," she said in a cold quiet bitter voice. "Though from the look in her eyes the one time I saw her close I would have said she would be the one to do the cutting or shooting."

"Nonsense," he said, hunching into his suspenders. "Nonsense." Because he was not talking to her now either. "Yes. The fool. To bring her here, of all places. To sealevel. To the Mississippi coast—Do you want me to put out the lamp?"

"Yes. You'll probably be there a long time if you are going to wait until you are paid." He blew out the lamp and descended the stairs again behind the torch. His black bag sat on the hall table beside his hat. The man Harry still stood just outside the front door.

"Maybe you better take this now," he said.

"What?" the doctor said. He paused, looking down, bringing the torch to bear on the single banknote in the other's extended hand. *Even if he has spent nothing, now he will have only fifteen dollars,* he thought. "No, later," he said. "Maybe we had better hurry." He bustled on ahead, following the torch's dancing beam, trotting while the other walked, across his own somewhat sheltered yard and through the dividing oleander hedge and so into the full sweep of the unimpeded seawind which thrashed among the unseen palms and hissed in the harsh salt grass of the unkempt other lot; now he could see a dim light in the other house. "Bleeding, hey?" he said. It was overcast; the invisible wind blew strong and steady among the invisible palms, from the invisible sea—a harsh steady sound full of the murmur of surf on the outside barrier islands, the spits and scars of sand bastioned with tossing and shabby pines. "Hemorrhage?"

"What?" the other said. "Hemorrhage?"

"No?" the doctor said. "She's just coughing a little blood then? Just spitting a little blood when she coughs, eh?"

"Spitting?" the other said. It was the tone, not the words. It was not addressed to the doctor and it was beyond laughter, as if that which it addressed were impervious to laughter; it was not the doctor who stopped; the doctor still trotted onward on his short sedentary legs, behind the jolting torch-beam, toward the dim waiting light, it was the Baptist, the provincial, who seemed to pause while the man, not the doctor now, thought not in shock but in a sort of despairing amazement: *Am I to live forever behind a barricade of perennial innocence like a chicken in a pen?* He spoke aloud quite carefully; the veil was going now, dissolving now, it was about to part now and now he did not want to see what was behind it; he knew that for the sake of his peace of mind forever afterward he did not dare and he knew that it was too late now and that he could not help himself; he heard his voice ask the question he did not want to ask and get the answer he did not want to hear:

"You say she is bleeding. Where is she bleeding?"

"Where do women bleed?" the other said, cried, in a harsh exasperated voice, not stopping. "I'm no doctor. If I were, do you think I would waste five dollars on you?"

Nor did the doctor hear this either. "Ah," he said. "Yes. I see. Yes." Now he stopped. He was aware of no cessation of motion since the steady dark wind still blew past him. *Because I am at the wrong age for this,* he thought. *If I were twenty-five I could say, Thank God I am not him because I would know it was only my luck today and that maybe tomorrow or next year it will be me and so I will not need to envy him. And if I were sixty-five I could say, Thank God, I am not him because then I would know I was too old for it to be possible and so it would not do me any good to envy him because he has proof on the body of love and of passion and of life that he is not dead. But now I am forty-eight and I did not think that I deserved this.* "Wait," he said; "wait." The other paused; they stood facing one another, leaning a little into the dark wind filled with the wild dry sound of the palms.

"I offered to pay you," the other said. "Isn't five enough? And if it isn't, will you give me the name of someone who will come for that and let me use your telephone?"

"Wait," the doctor said. *So Cofer was right,* he thought. *You are not married. Only why did you have to tell me so?* He didn't say that, of course, he said, "You haven't...You are not...What are you?"

The other, taller, leaned in the hard wind, looking down at the doctor with that impatience, that seething restraint. In the black wind the house, the shack, stood, itself invisible, the dim light shaped not by any door or window but rather like a strip of dim and forlorn bunting dingy and rigidly immobile in the wind. "What am I what?" he said. "I'm trying to be a painter. Is that what you mean?"

"A painter? But there is no building, no boom, no development here any more. That died nine years ago. You mean, you came here without any offer of work, any sort of contract at all?"

"I paint pictures," the other said. "At least, I think I do—
Well? Am I to use your phone or not?"

"You paint pictures," the doctor said; he spoke in that tone
of quiet amazement which thirty minutes later and then
tomorrow and tomorrow would vacillate among outrage and
anger and despair: "Well. She's probably still bleeding. Come
along." They went on. He entered the house first; even at the
moment he realized that he had preceded the other not as a
guest, not even as owner, but because he believed now that he
alone of the two of them had any right to enter it at all so long
as the woman was in it. They were out of the wind now. It
merely leaned, black, imponderable and firm, against the
door which the man called Harry had closed behind them:
and now and at once the doctor smelled again the odor of stale
and cooling gumbo. He even knew where it would be; he
could almost see it sitting uneaten (*They have not even tasted it,*
he thought. *But why should they? Why in God's name should
they?*) on the cold stove since he knew the kitchen well—the
broken stove, the spare cooking vessels, the meager collection
of broken knives and forks and spoons, the drinking recepta-
cles which had once contained gaudily labelled and machine-
made pickle and jam. He knew the entire house well, he
owned it, he had built it—the flimsy walls (they were not even
tongue-and-groove like the one in which he lived but were
of ship-lap, the synthetic joints of which, weathered and
warped by the damp salt air, leaked all privacy just as broken
socks and trousers do) murmurous with the ghosts of a thousand rented days and nights to which he (though not his wife)
had closed his eyes, insisting only that there be always an odd
number in any mixed party which stayed there overnight
unless the couple were strangers formally professing to be

man and wife, as now, even though he knew better and knew that his wife knew better. Because this was it, this the anger and outrage which would alternate with the despair tomorrow and tomorrow: *Why did you have to tell me?* he thought. *The others didn't tell me, upset me, didn't bring here what you brought, though I dont know what they might have taken away.*

At once he could see the dim lamplight beyond the open door. But he would have known which door without the light to guide him, the one beyond which the bed would be, the bed in which his wife said she would not ask a nigger servant to sleep; he could hear the other behind him and he realized for the first time that the man called Harry was still barefoot and that he was about to pass and enter the room first, thinking (the doctor) how he who actually had the only small portion of right to enter of either of them must hold back, feeling a dreadful desire to laugh, thinking, *You see, I dont know the etiquette in these cases because when I was young and lived in the cities where apparently such as this occurs, I suppose I was afraid, too afraid,* pausing because the other paused: so that it seemed to the doctor, in a steady silent glare of what he was never to know was actual clairvoyance, that they had both paused as if to allow the shade, the shadow, of the absent outraged rightful husband to precede them. It was a sound from within the room itself which moved them—the sound of a bottle against a glass.

"Just a minute," the man named Harry said. He entered the room quickly; the doctor saw, flung across the beach chair, the faded jeans that were too small for her in exactly the right places. But he did not move. He just heard the swift passage of the man's bare feet on the floor and then his voice, tense, not loud, quiet, quite gentle: so that suddenly the doctor believed he knew why there had been neither pain nor terror in the woman's face: that the man was carrying that too just as he carried the firewood and (doubtless) cooked with it the food she ate. "No, Charlotte," he said. "You mustn't. You cant. Come back to bed now."

"Why cant I?" the woman's voice said. "Why bloody cant I?" and now the doctor could hear them struggling. "Let me go, you bloody bungling bastard" (it was "rat," the noun, which the doctor believed he heard). "You promised, rat. That was all I asked and you promised. Because listen, rat—" the doctor could hear it, the voice cunning, secret now: "It wasn't him, you see. Not that bastard Wilbourne. I ratted off on him like I did you. It was the other one. You can't, anyway. I'll plead my ass like they used to plead their bellies and nobody ever knows just where the truth is about a whore to convict any-body—" The doctor could hear them, the two pairs of bare feet; it sounded as if they were dancing, furiously and infini-tesimally and without shoes. Then this stopped and the voice was not cunning, not secret. *But where's the despair?* the doctor thought. *Where's the terror?* "Jesus, there I went again. Harry! Harry! You promised."

"I've got you. It's all right. Come back to bed."

"Give me a drink."

"No. I told you no more. I told you why not. Do you hurt bad now?"

"Jesus, I dont know. I cant tell. Give me the drink, Harry. Maybe that will start it again."

"No. It cant now. It's too late for that to. Besides, the doc-tor's here now. He'll start it again. I'm going to put your gown on you so he can come in."

"And risk bloodying up the only nightgown I ever owned?"

"That's why. That's why we got the gown. Maybe that's all it will take to start it again. Come on now."

"Then why the doctor? Why the five dollars? Oh, you damned bloody bungling—No no no no. Quick. There I go again. Stop me quick. I am hurting. I cant help it. Oh, damn bloody bloody—" she began to laugh; it was hard laughing and not loud, like retching or coughing. "There. That's it. It's like dice. Come seven come eleven. Maybe if I can just keep on saying it—" He (the doctor) could hear them, the two pair of bare feet on the floor, then the rusty plaint of the bed springs, the woman still laughing, not loud, just with that abstract and furious despair which he had seen in her eyes over the bowl of gumbo at noon. He stood there, holding his little scuffed worn serviceable black bag, looking at the faded jeans among the wadded mass of other garments on the beach chair; he saw the man called Harry reappear and select from among them a nightgown and vanish again; the doctor looked at the chair. *Yes* he thought. *Just like the firewood.* Then the man called Harry was standing in the door.

"You can come in now," he said.

The Sacrifice

Kathleen Spivack

WHEN SHE FOUND OUT SHE WAS PREGNANT, SHE CALLED him up at the lab. "Guess what?" she said. She didn't wait for him to guess. She spoke into his silence. "I'm pregnant."

"What?" he said absently. He was holding a beaker up to a light.

"Guess what?" she repeated. "We are pregnant. We did it!" She wanted him to relate to the *We,* and the exclamation point.

"Hmm," he said, in his rough, fuzzy voice. He was cradling the phone in his chin, trying to free up both hands, swishing the liquid around in the bottle. He wished she wouldn't call him at work. He squinted at the fluid in the bottle, half on the phone, half not.

"Are you busy?" she asked, rather too late. "Maybe I should call back."

"No, no, it's okay," he said, tucking his ear to his shoulder. "What's up?"

She didn't want to start the conversation all over again. He had a bad habit of not listening. She felt her former enthusiasm go. It was an effort to repeat her news. A wave of irritation washed over her, but she forced herself to suppress it. After all, she was merely his girlfriend, not his wife. To the wife went the traits of bitchiness and anger.

She, the girlfriend, had chosen the accommodating, soft sweet role. "You are so gentle," he would murmur, kissing her ear. She never raised her voice to him, knowing instinctively that she would lose him if she expressed any normal female emotions or strength. She willingly had taken the light end of the seesaw, and the wife, like a great weight on the other end, went down, down, down. All the negative emotions slipped toward the wife, leaving Nancy light, free, and angelic, and Peter stood happily balanced at the mid-point. But a mistress doesn't have the rights of a wife, Nancy knew, and she felt strange calling him at his lab. That intrusion was the wifely prerogative. Nancy preferred to keep herself fresh and pure. She usually waited for Peter to call her. But now she could not contain herself.

Peter and Ellie had been married for ten years without children. "She doesn't want them," Peter had told Nancy, lying next to her in her careful fresh bed. "She is too interested in her career. We just don't get along." He sighed, nuzzling Nancy. "She says it's my fault." Nancy couldn't bear for Peter to feel bad for himself, and she rushed in like a nurse to reassure him. "You know you are so wonderful, I am sure it is not your fault." She felt a moment of righteous indignation toward her hard, career-driven rival, the wife.

"You know we don't sleep together anymore. She just doesn't seem to want to," he said. Nancy felt a triumphant pride in her own sexuality. She couldn't imagine not wanting to be with Peter. "You are so lovely," he told her, kissing the back of her knee.

Ellie, fresh out of business school, had taken a job that involved traveling. Peter had always traveled some for his job, but Ellie's absences gave him time to be with Nancy. He and

Nancy spent long stretches of days and nights together. The time was precious: snatched from the claws of routine and wife and work, it had a luxurious holiday feeling. In between, Nancy missed Peter and thought of him continually when he was not with her.

"She needs me," he explained to Nancy, returning to Ellie upon her return to town. "She would absolutely fall apart if I left her. I couldn't do that; I would feel too guilty."

Peter and Ellie had bought an old house in the East End and were fixing it up in their spare time. "It's ironic," he said, "the only thing we do together is tear down walls." Nancy pictured Ellie coming back from her business trips, putting down her briefcase, grabbing a hammer and attacking walls with great zest. She pictured Peter next to her. "We never talk," said Peter, kissing Nancy's breast. "It seems we both work so hard all the time." Nancy pictured Peter and Ellie at the end of the day marching off to separate rooms to hate each other. Why had they bought the house if they were thinking of splitting up? Nancy wondered. But Peter gave no explanation of that. "She wanted it," was all he would say.

Nancy's life was deceptively tidy and simple. She was a clean, light, quiet woman. She led an ordinary life. Her work was fairly low key. She worked as an assistant in a school art program. She had a tidy, orderly schedule with lots of time. Her hands were always cool and soothing. She and Peter had met in an evening photography course, and his dark, chaotic disorder and her light, untouchable cool had instantly attracted each other.

Nancy was delighted to be pregnant. She hadn't planned, hadn't consciously wanted it, but now the thought filled her with joy. When she first found out, Peter was out of town. She struggled with herself, unsure of what to do. Should she tell him? Nancy knew that part of her appeal to Peter lay in her independence. She did not want in any way to be a burden to him. She felt that to be a burden would be to diminish her sterling value; she would become "just another woman." She would become just like Ellie; in fact, she would have "made him" stay with her. He would resent her; she would lose him. Nancy wanted to whine, cling, throw her arms around him and have a tantrum every time Peter left her apartment to return to his wife. But she didn't allow herself to reveal even a flicker of that emotion, knowing instinctively that his freedom to come and go from her kept him in love with her. Nancy represented voluntary desire, not the dark, insistent bondage of his wife. Now Nancy wanted the child. She wanted Peter, the father, to be with her. She wanted to be a family.

"Of course you will have an abortion," Angela, Nancy's friend, said. "Do you want me to go with you?" But Nancy did not want an abortion; she wanted a child. And she wanted Peter.

"It is not fair not to tell him," Angela blinked her dark eyes earnestly, peering into Nancy's face. "He loves you. He would want to know."

"I would like to decide what to do first by myself," said Nancy; "I would feel better about it." When Nancy put on her smooth cool shell, no one dared to intrude. Angela withdrew, leaving Nancy to herself. But underneath the cool exterior Nancy seethed with emotion and confusion. She didn't know what to do. Was she prepared to have a child alone? There was a lot of feminist rhetoric to support it, but Nancy didn't quite feel capable of doing that.

She thought of her own parents. They were small and

blond and perfect, both of them now graying. They believed intensely in "the family." Nancy didn't see how she could face having a child alone, but maybe this would make Peter finally decide to leave Ellie. Nancy felt triumphant. After all, she was pregnant. Ellie was not. Yet she knew in her own cool appraisal that Peter would resent the pressure. Nancy looked at her own formerly slim body. Her stomach puffed out slightly. She had had two abortions earlier in her twenties. She couldn't bear going through that complicated physical and emotional upheaval again. She felt committed to Peter.

Peter, in his chemistry lab, was removed from all these concerns. He loved his work. He loved it for its own sake and also for the fact that it drowned out the women in his life. When he was at work nothing mattered except the systems he was working with. Basically, people's emotions irritated him, except when he chose to seek them out. He loved the gleam of the equipment, the bubbling chemicals, the reactions he could create and observe, and the objective working of his mind upon problems. Peter admired efficiency and intelligence. It was what had drawn him to his wife in the first place and what he perceived in Nancy's calm beauty. It was when women became emotional that Peter felt intruded upon. Here in the lab he could control what happened. If in the course of chemistry a new discovery showed itself to be something for which no controls had been prepared, that was data, interesting data, and Peter's mind sprang into mathematical analysis.

So he was irritated when the phone rang. He had had his concentration disturbed. He always answered the phone, that annoying intrusion, with an irritated bark to put the caller off, to force the caller to state his business quickly and hang up so that Peter could get back to his chemicals. He was so impatient with the phone that often he didn't even get what was being said to him.

"We are pregnant," Nancy was saying with false gaiety. Nancy herself finally registered on the outermost circle of Peter's consciousness. He pictured her: calm and lovely and welcoming, her stomach swelling up. For a moment he thought she was Ellie. Ellie who wanted children so badly. Ellie was the model of dark, tidy efficiency with her briefcase, her meetings, her success in her firm. But Ellie had gone to doctor after doctor trying to understand why she could not conceive. She had dragged Peter with her too. "But, Ellie," Peter had said kindly in his abstracted way, putting his large hands on her small, taut shoulders, "we don't need children. We have each other." "And our work," he had continued gently. "You could never work as hard as you do and take care of a child."

Quiet tears had rolled down Ellie's face. "It is okay," he had said, kissing her, "it is okay." He had held her small, tight, determined body tenderly.

Peter had wondered if their infertility was his fault. He hadn't dared admit to Ellie that he worried. He hadn't dared to ask the doctor either, and the whole inquiry into their infertility was distasteful and embarrassing to him. How he'd resented Ellie for dragging him through it! On the surface Peter would have done anything for his wife. He admired her drive and determination, her beautiful fighting spirit. But he had had the indignity and humiliation of their continuing infertility forced on him by Ellie's desire for a child. His times with Nancy had been a refuge for him. A place where he was accepted and admired simply as a man and a lover.

"Pregnant, huh?" he said now to Nancy. It was beginning to dawn on him. He felt a bubble of delight well up in him. So it hadn't been his fault after all. He *could* get a woman pregnant. He could have a son. A large smile split Peter's face.

"That's wonderful," he said to Nancy, "that's wonderful." He put down the flask suddenly, taking the phone in both hands, focusing now on the fact that he, Peter, was to be a father. "That's wonderful." A wave of joy and relief washed over him, sweeping him up. He was speaking not to Nancy, not to Ellie, but to women in general; he, Peter, a man, a father.

"What will we name him?" he asked Nancy, starting to laugh. It was going to be a *him*. Nancy was overcome with relief herself. "I have decided to have it," she told Peter. But Peter was caught up in his fantasy of naming the child. "Listen, I will call you back," Peter said. He put down the phone abruptly.

He suddenly could not speak. He was overcome with turmoil: delight, confusion, and guilt struggled within him. Peter turned back to his experiment, but he could not concentrate. He could not recapture the solitary happiness of the formulae or the serenity and peace that he had felt in the lab. He picked up and put down equipment. He thought of Ellie sitting in a board meeting in a city far away looking dark and elegant and intelligent, hiding her insecurities. Only he, Peter, knew them. He had married her, he had made a commitment. No one else could understand the fierce, trapped love he and Ellie had for each other. Two cool, willful, intelligent animals, determined to stick together and see it out. They shared a savage joy in remodeling their house, fiercely pursuing their careers and doing exactly what they wanted; determined to rise above the humiliation of childlessness.

Peter then thought of Nancy, cool and blonde and efficient. Nancy was not one for tears and storms. How he admired that. "She will be okay," he murmured. His eyes glinted with pride for Nancy, confident and self-contained. He had never seen her desperate, and he respected her. But a child? No, he really could not face starting a family that way. He simply didn't want to. He wasn't going to. Nobody was going to make him. Nancy knew the risks when she got involved with him, he thought. No, I simply couldn't, it wouldn't do, there was no way. His inner voice was getting stronger. No way he was going to be forced into a relationship with Nancy, no way. "No way," he said aloud. His relief at proof of his own fertility was enough, his knowledge that he could conceive a child. "Wait till I tell Ellie," he thought; "she will never blame me again." But then with a pain he realized he could never tell Ellie. It would kill her, he thought. She would never survive.

Quickly he turned back to the phone and dialed Nancy's number. He crouched over the phone, holding it close to his body, speaking urgently into the mouthpiece. "Hi, Nancy," he said.

"Oh, hi." Her calm voice could not hide its surge of happiness.

"Listen, Nance," Peter said. "I am in a tough spot. I can't deal with this. It is too much for me. I don't care what you do. You work it out any way you want. If you need money, let me know. I just can't deal with this. I can't face telling Ellie. I can't deal with this. I will send you a check, just you go and do what you want. I just don't want to know about it." Peter leaned again into the phone. It had been one of his longer speeches. He felt drained. There was silence on the other end as Nancy tried to comprehend what Peter was saying.

"Look, I know it is rotten of me, but I just don't want to know about it. I can't deal with it. Do what you want," he repeated.

He thought of Ellie, small and defeated, flying back on a plane to him. He would always be tied to Ellie by his secret.

He was allowing his child, Nancy's child, to be sacrificed. Ellie would never know, but Peter would have a secret hold on her forever, and the price was Nancy, whom Peter would give up. He would commit himself to Ellie anew, his marriage bought by the terrible double sacrifice: Nancy and the child.

"Nance, look," he said, "I know you will be okay." He was shaking, for he knew he was saying goodbye to Nancy. He knew he was being a cad, but he could not help himself. Nancy could not speak for alarm and terror.

"Hey, Nance," he said, "I'm sorry." His words were inadequate. "I'm sorry. I really am. You are a wonderful girl." Nancy did not answer, and Peter spoke firmly into her silence.

"I know you will be okay," he repeated. "I know you will be just fine."

Beg, Sl Tog, Inc, Cont, Rep

Amy Hempel

THE MOHAIR WAS SCRATCHY, THE STRIA TOO BULKY, but the homespun tweed was right for a small frame. I bought slate-blue skeins softened with flecks of pink, and size-10 needles for a sweater that was warm but light. The pattern I chose was a two-tone V-neck with an optional six-stitch cable up the front. Pullovers mess the hair, but I did not want to buttonhole the first time out.

From a needlework book, I learned to cast on. In the test piece, I got the gauge and correct tension. Knit and purl came naturally, as though my fingers had been rubbed in spiderwebs at birth. The sliding of the needles was as rhythmic as water.

Learning to knit was the obvious thing. The separation of tangled threads, the working-together of raveled ends into something tangible and whole—this *mending* was as confounding as the groom who drives into a stop sign on the way to his wedding. Because symptoms mean just what they are. What about the woman whose empty hand won't close because she cannot grasp that her child is gone?

"Would you get me a Dr Pep, gal, and would you turn up the a-c?"

I put down my knitting. In the kitchen I found some sugar-free, and took it, with ice, to Dale Anne. It was August. Air-conditioning lifted her hair as she pressed the button on the Niagara bed. Dr. Diamond insisted she have it the last month. She was also renting a swivel TV table and a vibrating chaise—the Niagara adjustable home.

When the angle was right, she popped a Vitamin E and rubbed the oil where the stretch marks would be.

I could be doing this, too. But I had had the procedure instead. That was after the father had asked me, Was I sure? To his credit, he meant—sure that I *was,* not sure was it he. He said he had never made a girl pregnant before. He said that he had never even made a girl late.

I moved in with Dale Anne to help her near the end. Her husband is often away—in a clinic or in a lab. He studies the mind. He is not a doctor yet, but we call him one by way of encouragement.

I had picked up a hank of yarn and was winding it into a ball when the air-conditioner choked to a stop.

Dale Anne sighed. "I will *cook* in this robe. Would you get me that flowered top in the second drawer?"

While I looked for the top, Dale Anne twisted her hair and held it tight against her head. She took one of my double-pointed six-inch needles and wove it in and out of her hair, securing the twist against her scalp. With the hair off her face, she looked wholesome and very young—"the person you would most like to go camping with if you couldn't have sex," is how she put it.

I turned my back while Dale Anne changed. She was as modest as I was. If the house caught fire one night, we would both die struggling to hook brassieres beneath our gowns.

I went back to my chair, and as I did, a sensational cramp snapped me over until I was nearly on the floor.

"Easy, gal—what's the trouble?" Dale Anne started out of bed to come see.

I said it sometimes happens since the procedure, and Dale Anne said, "Let's not talk about that for at *least* ten years."

I could not think of what to say to that. But I didn't have to. The front door opened, earlier than it usually did. It was Dr. Diamond, home from the world of spooks and ghosts and loony bins and Ouija boards. I knew that a lack of concern for others was a hallmark of mental illness, so I straightened up and said, after he'd kissed his pregnant wife, "You look hot, Dr. Diamond. Can I get you a drink?"

I buy my materials at a place in the residential section. The owner's name is Ingrid. She is a large Norwegian woman who spells needles "kneedles." She wears sample knits she makes up for the class demonstrations. The vest she wore the day before will be hanging in the window.

There are always four or five women at Ingrid's round oak table, knitting through a stretch they would not risk alone.

Often I go there when I don't need a thing. In the small back room that is stacked high with pattern books, I can sift for hours. I scan the instructions abbreviated like musical notation: *K10, sl 1, K2 tog, psso, sl 1, K10 to end.* I feel I could *sing* these instructions. It is compression of language into code; your ability to decipher it makes you privy to the secrets shared by Ingrid and the women at the round oak table.

In the other room, Ingrid tells a customer she used to knit two hundred stitches a minute.

I scan the French and English catalogues, noting the longer length of coat. There is so much to absorb on each visit.

Mary had a little lamb, I am humming when I leave the shop. *Its feet were—its fleece was white as wool.*

Dale Anne wanted a nap, so Dr. Diamond and I went out for margaritas. At La Rondalla, the colored lights on the Virgin tell you every day is Christmas. The food arrives on manhole covers and mariachis fill the bar. Dr. Diamond said that in Guadalajara there is a mariachi college that turns out mariachis by the classful. But I could tell that these were not graduates of even mariachi high school.

I shooed the serenaders away, but Dr. Diamond said they meant well.

Dr. Diamond likes for people to mean well. He could be president of the Well-Meaning Club. He has had a buoyant feeling of fate since he learned Freud died the day he was born.

He was the person to talk to, all right, so I brought up the stomach pains I was having for no bodily reason that I could think of.

"You know how I think," he said. "What is it you can't stomach?"

I knew what he was asking.

"Have you thought about how you will feel when Dale Anne has the baby?" he asked.

With my eyes, I wove strands of tinsel over the Blessed Virgin. That was the great thing about knitting, I thought—everything was fiber, the world a world of natural resource.

"I thought I would burn that bridge when I come to it," I said, and when he didn't say anything to that, I said, "I guess I will think that there is a mother who *kept* hers."

"*One* of hers might be more accurate," Dr. Diamond said.

*

172

I arrived at the yarn shop as Ingrid turned over the *Closed* sign to *Open*. I had come to buy Shetland wool for a Fair Isle sweater. I felt nothing would engage my full attention more than a pattern of ancient Scottish symbols and alternate bands of delicate design. Every stitch in every color is related to the one above, below, and to either side.

I chose the natural colors of Shetland sheep—the chalky brown of the Moorit, the blackish brown of the black sheep, fawn, gray, and pinky beige from a mixture of Moorit and white. I held the wool to my nose, but Ingrid said it was fifty years since the women of Fair Isle dressed the yarn with fish oil.

She said the yarn came from Sheep Rock, the best pasture on Fair Isle. It is a ten-acre plot that is four hundred feet up a cliff, Ingrid said. "Think what a man has to go through to harvest the wool."

I was willing to feel an obligation to the yarn, and to the hardy Scots who supplied it. There was heritage there, and I could keep it alive with my hands.

Dale Anne patted capers into a mound of raw beef, and spread some onto toast. It was not a pretty sight. She offered some to me, and I said not a chance. I told her Johnny Carson is someone else who won't go near that. I said, "Johnny says he won't eat steak tartare because he has seen things hurt worse than that get better."

"Johnny was never pregnant," Dale Anne said.

When the contractions began, I left a message with the hospital and with Dr. Diamond's lab. I turned off the air-conditioner and called for a cab.

"Look at you," Dale Anne said.

I told her I couldn't help it. I get rational when I panic.

The taxi came in minutes.

"Hold on," the driver said. "I know every bump in these roads, and I've never been able to miss one of them."

Dale Anne tried to squeeze my wrist, but her touch was weightless, as porous as wet silk.

"When this is over…" Dale Anne said.

When the baby was born, I did not go far. I sublet a place on the other side of town. I filled it with patterns and needles and yarn. It was what I did in the day. On a good day, I made a front and two sleeves. On a bad day, I ripped out stitches from neck to hem. For variety, I made socks. The best ones I made had beer steins on the sides, and the tops spilled over with white angora foam.

I did not like to work with sound in the room, not even the sound of a fan. Music slowed me down, and there was a great deal to do. I planned to knit myself a mailbox and a car, perhaps even a dog and a lead to walk him.

I blocked the finished pieces and folded them in drawers.

Dr. Diamond urged me to exercise. He called from time to time, looking in. He said exercise would set me straight, and why not have some fun with it? Why not, for example, tap-dancing lessons?

I told him it would be embarrassing because the rest of the class would be doing it right. And with all the knitting, there wasn't time to dance.

Dale Anne did not look in. She had a pretty good reason not to.

The day I went to see her in the hospital, I stopped at the nursery first. I saw the baby lying face down. He wore yellow duck-print flannels. I saw that he was there—and then I went straight home.

That night the dreams began. A giant lizard ate people from the feet upwards, swallowing the argyles on the first bite, then drifting into obscurity like a ranger of forgotten death. I woke up remembering and, like a chameleon, assumed every shade of blame.

Asleep at night, I went to an elegant ball. In the center of the dance floor was a giant aquarium. Hundreds of goldfish swam inside. At a sign from the bandleader, the tank was overturned. Until someone tried to dance on the fish, the floor was aswirl with gold glory.

Dr. Diamond told a story about the young daughter of a friend. The little girl had found a frog in the yard. The frog appeared to be dead, so her parents let her prepare a burial site—a little hole surrounded by pebbles. But at the moment of the lowering, the frog, which had only been stunned, kicked its legs and came to.

"Kill him!" the girl had shrieked.

I began to take walks in the park. In the park, I saw a dog try to eat his own shadow, and another dog—I am sure of it— was herding a stand of elms. I stopped telling people how handsome their dogs were; too many times what they said was, "You want him?"

When the weather got nicer, I stayed home to sit for hours.

I had accidents. Then I had bigger ones. But the part that hurt was never the part that got hurt.

The dreams came back and back until they were just— again. I wished that things would stay out of sight the way they did in mountain lakes. In one that I know, the water is so cold, gas can't form to bring a corpse to the surface. Although you would not want to think about the bottom of the lake, what you can say about it is—the dead stay down.

Around that time I talked to Dr. Diamond.

The point that he wanted to make was this: that conception was not like walking in front of traffic. No matter now badly timed, it was, he said, an affirmation of life.

"You have to believe me here," he said. "Do you see that this is true? Do you know this about yourself?"

"I do and I don't," I said.

"You do and you *do,*" he said.

I remembered when another doctor made the news. A young retarded boy had found his father's gun, and while the family slept, he shot them all in bed. The police asked the boy what he had done. But the boy went mute. He told them nothing. Then they called in the doctor.

"We know *you* didn't do it," the doctor said to the boy, "but tell me, did the *gun* do it?"

And yes, the boy was eager to tell him just what that gun had done.

I wanted the same out, and Dr. Diamond wouldn't let me have it.

"Dr. Diamond," I said, "I am giving up."

"Now you are ready to begin," he said.

I thought of Andean alpaca because that was what I planned to work up next. The feel of that yarn was not the only wonder—there was also the name of it: Alpaquita Superfina.

Dr. Diamond was right.

I was ready to begin.

Beg, sl tog, inc, cont, rep.

Begin, slip together, increase, continue, repeat.

*

Dr. Diamond answered the door. He said Dale Anne had run to the store. He was leaving, too, flying to a conference back East. The baby was asleep, he said, I should make myself at home.

I left my bag of knitting in the hall and went into Dale Anne's kitchen. It had been a year. I could have looked in on the baby. Instead, I washed the dishes that were soaking in the sink. The scouring pad was steel wool waiting for knitting needles.

The kitchen was filled with specialized utensils. When Dale Anne couldn't sleep she watched TV, and that's where the stuff was advertised. She had a thing to core tomatoes—it was called a Tomato Shark—and a metal spaghetti wheel for measuring out spaghetti. She had plastic melon-ballers and a push-in device that turned ordinary cake into ladyfingers.

I found pasta primavera in the refrigerator. My fingers wanted to knit the cold linguini, laying precisely cabled strands across the oily red peppers and beans.

Dale Anne opened the door.

"*Look* out, gal," she said, and dropped a shopping bag on the counter.

I watched her unload ice cream, potato chips, carbonated drinks, and cake.

"It's been a long time since I walked into a market and expressed myself," she said.

She turned to toss me a carton of cigarettes.

"Wait for me in the bedroom," she said. "*West Side Story* is on."

I went in and looked at the color set. I heard the blender crushing ice in the kitchen. I adjusted the contrast, then Dale Anne handed me an enormous peach daiquiri. The goddamn thing had a tide factor.

Dale Anne left the room long enough to bring in the take-out chicken. She upended the bag on a plate and picked out a leg and a wing.

"I like my dinner in a bag and my life in a box," she said, nodding toward the TV.

We watched the end of the movie, then part of a lame detective program. Dale Anne said the show *owed* Nielsen four points, and reached for the *TV Guide*.

"Eleven-thirty," she read. *"The Texas Whiplash Massacre:* Unexpected stop signs were their weapon."

"Give me that," I said.

Dale Anne said there was supposed to be a comet. She said we could probably see it if we watched from the living room. Just to be sure, we pushed the couch up close to the window. With the lights off, we could see everything without it seeing us. Although both of us had quit, we smoked at either end of the couch.

"Save my place," Dale Anne said.

She had the baby in her arms when she came back in. I looked at the sleeping child and thought, Mercy, Land Sakes, Lordy Me. As though I had aged fifty years. For just a moment then I wanted nothing that I had and everything I did not.

"He told his first joke today," Dale Anne said.

"What do you mean he told a joke?" I said. "I didn't think they could talk."

"Well, he didn't really *tell* a joke—he poured his orange juice over his head, and when I started after him, he said, 'Raining?'"

"'Raining?' That's what he said? The kid is a genius," I told Dale Anne. "What Art Linkletter could do with this kid."

Dale Anne laid him down in the middle of the couch, and we watched him or watched the sky.

*

"What a gyp," Dale Anne said at dawn.

There had not been a comet. But I did not feel cheated, or even tired. She walked me to the door.

The knitting bag was still in the hall.

"Open it later," I said. "It's a sweater for him."

But Dale Anne had to see it then.

She said the blue one matched his eyes and the camel one matched his hair. The red would make him glow, she said, and then she said, "Help me out."

Cables had become too easy; three more sweaters had pictures knitted in. They buttoned up the front. Dale Anne held up a parade of yellow ducks.

There were the Fair Isles, too—one in the pattern called Tree of Life, another in the pattern called Hearts.

It was an excess of sweaters—a kind of precaution, a rehearsal against disaster.

Dale Anne looked at the two sweaters still in the bag. "Are you really okay?" she said.

The worst of it is over now, and I can't say that I am glad. Lose that sense of loss—you have gone and lost something else. But the body moves toward health. The mind, too, in steps. One step at a time. Ask a mother who has just lost a child, How many children do you have? "Four," she will say, "—three," and years later, "Three," she will say, "—four."

It's the little steps that help. Weather, breakfast, crossing with the light—sometimes it is all the pleasure I can bear to sleep, and know that on a rack in the bath, damp wool is pinned to dry.

Dale Anne thinks she would like to learn to knit. She measures the baby's crib and I take her over to Ingrid's. Ingrid steers her away from the baby pastels, even though they are machine-washable. Use a pure wool, Ingrid says. Use wool in a grown-up shade. And don't boast of your achievements or you'll be making things for the neighborhood.

On Fair Isle there are only five women left who knit. There is not enough lichen left growing on the island for them to dye their yarn. But knitting machines can't produce their designs, and they keep on, these women, working the undyed colors of the sheep.

I wait for Dale Anne in the room with the patterns. The songs in these books are like lullabies to me.

K tog rem st. Knit together remaining stitches.

Cast off loosely.

Contributors

RICHARD BRAUTIGAN (1935–1984) earned a reputation in the 1960s as an American novelist and poet. His books include *The Pill Versus the Springhill Mine Disaster, Rommel Drives on Deep into Egypt, A Confederate General from Big Sur, Trout Fishing in America, In Watermelon Sugar,* and *Revenge of the Lawn.*

BABS H. DEAL grew up in the South and attended the University of Alabama. Her works include *Acres of Afternoon, It's Always Three O'Clock,* and *Night Story.*

JOAN DIDION is a noted essayist and novelist whose books are *Run River, Play It As It Lays, A Book of Common Prayer, Slouching Towards Bethlehem, The White Album, Salvador, Democracy, Essays and Interviews,* and *Miami.* She is married to John Gregory Dunne.

ZÖE FAIRBAIRNS studied at St. Andrews University and the College of William and Mary. Her publications include novels, short stories, poetry, and political commentary. She was part of a collaborative writing effort that produced the book *Tales I Tell My Mother.* She lives in London.

WILLIAM FAULKNER (1897–1962) was one of America's foremost novelists. His works include *The Sound and the Fury, As I Lay Dying, Light in August, The Hamlet,* and *Go Down, Moses.* He was awarded the Nobel Prize for literature in 1949.

ELLEN GILCHRIST was born in Mississippi and educated at Vanderbilt University and Millsaps College. Her books of short fiction include *In the Land of Dreamy Dreams, Victory Over Japan* (which won a National Book Award), *Drunk in Love,* and *Light Can Be Both Wave and Particle.* Her novels are *The Annunciation* and *The Anna Papers.* She has also written poetry, novellas, and a collection of journal entries, *Falling Through Space.*

AMY HEMPEL was born in Chicago and now lives in New York. She is the author of two short story collections, *Reasons to Live* and *At the Gates of the Animal Kingdom.*

LANGSTON HUGHES (1902–1967) was one of the important figures of the Harlem Renaissance and had a big hand in the development of Afro-American literature. He wrote two volumes of autobiography; *The Big Sea* and *I Wonder as I Wander,* as well as numerous poetry collections: *The Weary Blues, Shakespeare in Harlem, Ask Your Mama,* and *The Panther and the Lash.* His other books include *Simple Speaks His Mind, Tambourines to Glory,* and *The Ways of White Folks.*

AUDRE LORDE (1934–1992) was born and raised in New York of Grenadian parents. She was educated at the National University of Mexico, Hunter College, and Columbia University. Her poetic work includes *The New York Head Shop and Museum, Coal, The Black Unicorn,* and *Our Dead Behind Us.* Her prose includes *The Cancer Journals, Sister Outsider,* and *Burst of Light.*

GLORIA NAYLOR was born in New York and graduated from Brooklyn College and Yale University. Among her best-known novels are *The Women of Brewster Place, Linden Hills, Mama Day,* and *Bailey's Cafe.*

FYODOR SOLOGUB (1863–1927) was the pen name of Fyodor Kuzmich Teternikov, a Russian novelist and short story writer. Sologub was a schoolteacher until the success of *The Little Demon* allowed him to devote himself to writing. Other books include *Bad Dreams* and *The Created Legend.*

KATHLEEN SPIVACK directs the Advanced Writing Workshop in Cambridge, Massachusetts. She is the author of several poetry books, including *Flying Island, The Jane Poems, Swimmer in the Spreading Dawn,* and *The Beds We Lie In: New and Selected Poems,* and the short story collection *The Honeymoon.*

CAROLINE THOMPSON grew up in Bethesda, Maryland. Her novel, *First Born,* was published in 1983. Since then she has gone on to earn screenwriting credits for *Edward Scissorhands, The Addams Family, Homeword Bound: The Incredible Journey, The Secret Garden,* and to write and direct *Black Beauty.*

ALICE WALKER is one of the most important fiction writers in America today. Her books include *The Third Life of Grange Copeland, Meridian, You Can't Keep a Good Woman Down, The Color Purple* (which won the 1983 Pulitzer Prize), and *Possessing the Secret of Joy.*

BOOK DESIGN AND PREPARATION BY CHARLES NIX